MEMORY'S
HOSTAGE

MARGARET PINARD

TASTE LIFE TWICE PUBLISHING
Memory's Hostage
Margaret Pinard

Published in the United States by Taste Life Twice Publish-
ing
ISBN 978-0-9898506-6-7
Version 5

FOR GINNY

Also by Margaret Pinard

Dulci's Legacy

The Keening

The Grasping Root

To Sheila a
(Margaret)
a very good
neighbor...
(do tell me
the things I
got wrong!) ☺

MEMORY'S

HOSTAGE

Margit Dal
12-3-17

Taste Life Twice Publishing

Chapter 1

She awoke in her mind.

She heard ringing, and dreamily wondered whether it had to do with her, and why it wasn't a clearer sound.

Sounds drifted past her in the same dream-like state. Was that a muffled voice? After a few more idle thoughts wandered past, she started to grow agitated. Why wasn't the ringing connected to a vibration? Why wasn't the voice linked to a face? Why wasn't she feeling anything with her body, or through her other senses?

Panic started to flutter within her, startling her thoughts back into her body. She gradually registered water lapping at her sides, her arms underneath and behind her, and her eyes heavily closed. She struggled to open them, lifting what felt like weights from her lashes. She could now see she was in a bathtub full of water, with no clothes, and no idea how she had got there.

Her mind seemed to hit a brick wall as she tried to remember what had happened prior to this moment, and nothing came—no faces, no catastrophic events. She could feel her heart beating rapidly as she tried to reason with herself, panic taking the form of a lump in her throat, threatening to block any air from coming in.

But at the very least, I know what faces are, what a bathtub is. I have not lost all knowledge of the world, she thought.

Just memory, her mind echoed. The lump in her throat seemed to liquefy and drown her; she tried to push it away with logic. She cleared her throat with difficulty and felt her body tingle with renewed awareness.

Logic, she thought. Use your brain. She felt something tied around her elbows, keeping them behind her. She lay in a porcelain bathtub full of water up to her chin. And she was naked. She spied a window with a wooden screen, and her mind reached out to it like a beacon—*Window*. After observing all that she could without moving, she paused to still her thoughts, forcing the worry and doubt into a physical effort to push with her legs, easing her body up the back of the tub to look around.

As her head reached the edge, she saw that she was in a small bathroom with wood-paneled walls, a washstand, a richly colored rug, a shelf for towels, a mirror–*Mirror*. She felt another sensation of tingling, of knowing without being able to follow the thought. It was maddening. What had happened to her memory? And why was she bound? Had she become both lunatic and amnesiac after some awful event?

She paused again to quiet the panic that threatened. Concentrate on getting to that window.

Well, she thought, it's up to me. I am a strong, practical young woman from—

Where was she from? And where was she now?

.

Chapter 2

Henry MacFarlane folded his letters and placed them on the open secretary, taking his seal out to secure them and then writing the direction. His thoughts were far away with concern for his brother Horace, who was constantly in need of rescuing from situations of his own making. Right now his brother was no doubt recovering from a full night at the gaming tables of London, even though his trip was for the express purpose of delivering an answer to a valued customer of the firm.

Henry sighed, rising to finish his morning toilette. He picked up his comb, opened the door to his bathroom, and beheld the extraordinary sight of a naked young woman, her hands tied behind her back, on tiptoe in front of his window, angling to see around the wooden window screen.

He jolted to a stop at the sight of her, rapping his knuckles on the washstand, and she whipped around with wide eyes staring, her hands flat against the wall at her back. Neither said anything.

After a few shocked moments, Henry regained his composure enough to make a hastly guess that she must be the victim of some horrid trick being played or even a crime from her expression of fear. He grasped a towel and with a downcast look offered to wrap it over her.

"Yes," he heard her whisper. He gingerly placed the insufficient towel around the young woman's neck; it hung down to her thighs. He was trying not to touch her with his hands as he held the towel in place, puzzled how to proceed, when she slowly turned her back to him. Henry saw the strips of linen around her elbows and realized he should do this first: untie her arms. She must be extremely uncomfortable. He struggled again not to look at the round bottom below her wrists, the pale legs.

"So sorry," he murmured. "There you are," he continued as he took his shaving razor from the washstand drawer and sawed through the cloth neatly. He went back into his bedroom, retrieved a stool and a quilt, pulled the cord to call a servant, and returned to the bathroom. Placing the stool next to the woman's legs, he offered the quilt to her as she sat slowly, clutching it around herself and looking down at her hands with intense concentration.

"I have called a servant who will fetch the police. We will find some clothes for you, and then the police will be able to take care of you." He paused as she did not stir, and then said, "Madam, I am extremely sorry to have found you in such a state of—shock, and distress—I have no idea how you came to be in my house in that—in such a—goodness."

The young woman observed his being quite out of countenance, and said, "You mean, you haven't done this to me?"

Her voice was timid and uncertain, but deliberately low-pitched, as if to nail down any inclination to go spinning off into space. Henry was floored at the question. He worried that if the girl had no memory of what had happened to her, the police he would call would likely suspect him of doing her ill. Time to establish facts.

* * *

"I am Henry MacFarlane," he was saying, "and I have no idea how you got here or what happened to you before this very minute." She was somehow not surprised at this, even though her logical conclusion upon his entrance had been that this must be her captor. His astonishment and subsequent embarrassment showed her that he could not have been familiar with her. She clung to the self-assertion that she was a sensible young woman, and raised her eyes to his.

"I do not at present know what my name is, nor do I know how I came to be here beyond a few moments ago. I think—I think my name may be

Alice, though." She paused, unsure of how to proceed. "I woke up in the bath without any memory, as you saw me, and I have been trying to deduce what has happened, but I cannot get very far. If you also know nothing, then that is very puzzling. Can you tell me at least where we are?"

"That I can; you are in Atwell, my family's home in Tidewater, in Carknocke County," he replied. "England," he added, in case it was needed. But no, she knew nothing of Carknocke County, so the information only puzzled her.

She was familiar with England, its accents, its people, but felt no connection to a particular corner of it. First, no name; now, no home.

* * *

As the woman possibly named Alice frowned in thought, a servant arrived, a white-haired gentleman in black. He stood inside the door, allowing the sight of the young, still-wet woman now swaddled in the young master's bed quilt to widen his eyes perceptibly before he turned to his master and waited.

"Arthur, please fetch some clothes suitable for this young lady. She has just been found here stranded and in some distress, and we are trying to discover how this may have occurred. Do you have any knowledge of this?"

He eyed the older man passively, sure that he would have nothing to contribute to this mystery, not disappointed by the servant's apologetic shake of the head and his reply, "No, sir. Shall I call the police then, sir?"

Henry was going to say yes, after the clothes, but turned to the girl to confirm that is what she wished. She was still frowning into the air. It looked like she was trying hard to remember something. "Yes, Arthur, thank you," he said.

He turned back and asked, "Miss Alice, then, would you like to sit in the other room while you wait for a set of clothes? I can be quite out of the way while you wait for the police. It should not be long; these are clothes of my mother's that are not being used. Excuse me, I should have asked, are you thirsty? Hungry? Anything else I can bring for your ease?"

The frowning increased the lines on her forehead until she looked up, and he realized she was making a supreme effort not to shed the tears already waiting in her eyes.

"Excuse me," he murmured, and ducked out of the bathroom, clearing the bedroom as well.

* * *

It was all very overwhelming. Thoughts were buzzing in and out of her mind, and she tried to marshal them into order, but she also had to deal with what was going on outside her mind: this man, this house, and this new nothingness. She rose from the stool, retaining the towel and quilt, and trod slowly into the bedroom, gazing about unabashed without the presence of its owner. She let the tears fall.

She had not felt one of those surging sensations when he had said "Alice," and yet there had been something that nudged that name at her. She did not know anything of Tidewater or Carknocke County, but was familiar with England. She did not recognize this man named Henry but did not feel threatened by him either. She felt an altogether detached sense of being, where her physical senses were sharpened, but the messages they sent her appeared to be nothing but confusion, and were no help in determining how to handle this situation.

Was she in danger? Or out of it?

Chapter 3

Henry knocked at his bedroom door, heard nothing, and waited. After a moment, the door was opened by the young woman, who was now dressed in an old dress of his mother's and boots of an old servant, her hair dried and pulled back. It looked wilder this way, as it was vibrantly curly and a lighter reddish color than what he could see when it was wet. She was of average height for a girl of twenty or so, and had a good figure, which he had tried not to notice when he had first come upon her. Well, then, he would call her Alice—until something else was settled upon.

"Miss Alice," he began, "have you remembered anything else?" He tried to be direct, as he sensed she needed to be appealed to in an honest manner, rather than coddled or tricked, as Lord knew she had probably already been victimized somehow. His stomach turned at the thought of what might have happened to this girl, now that he could see her as an ordinary person instead of some meek invader of his bathroom.

The directness of his question did not faze her because, he realized, she had been expecting it and had braced to answer, "No. Could you tell me any more of this place? It might help."

He watched her features closely as he made some remarks about his family, their time in the neighborhood, and his occupation. He noted that nothing he said elicited a visible response from her, and he felt somewhat dispirited, but also relieved that maybe this meant that nothing about the crime concerned his family, vulnerable as they were to scandal.

She sensed he was watching her as she took in the information, so she kept her gaze on the floor. "My family, the MacFarlanes, have been here for several generations. My grandfather built this house for his wife after their marriage when nothing existed in the area, in the early Twenties. As the coal mines west of here grew in importance, my father participated in some of the rail interests that shipped coal to the Continent. I currently manage some aspects of the trade concerns, but also hold an active position on several boards of directors of private companies having to do with industrial policies in Britain and the Empire. I know very little about amnesiac cases, but I am sure the police will be able to consult with very capable doctors in determining the best way to help you retrieve your memory, if it does not come back on its own, as it may well do in a few days."

The young lady tipped forward as if falling, even though she was sitting in his desk chair; he caught her arm and looked into her face to see whether she was still conscious, but she was wearing that frowning expression again, intensely concentrating on something. Was she remembering? Was she trying not to remember? He let go of her arm gently, and asked, "Are you all right? Can I do anything for you—fetch some wine? You have likely not eaten in some time."

She looked at him, struggling to keep her face clear of the torment within, and released a held breath. She said, "I am a bit afraid of the police, although I'm not sure why I should be. There was something when you said that—I don't know, perhaps a memory. I do hope it comes back soon. I feel utterly unable to think about—" She stood up, fortitude shining from an intent face. She made a noise like a cough cut off midway, her eyes rolled back, and her strength abruptly deserted her.

* * *

When she next awoke, she was in a bed with the covers drawn up to her chin, which made her unbearably uncomfortable. She pushed them down, sat up, and saw there was another young woman, a servant, in the room, watching her.

"I'm Mary, miss, and I'm to ask if you require anything."

"No, I am all right for the moment. I—thank you."

Mary spoke again. "The police have arrived as well, and are speaking with Master Henry now, but want to speak with you in time. A doctor has also been called, I was told to tell you."

"Thank you, yes, that is all right. I will speak with the police when they are ready; there is not much I can tell them."

Mary looked at her queerly, as if she wasn't sure whether to believe her or not, but then bobbed her head and left the room.

She was not in the master bedroom, that room in which she had fainted what must have been more than a few moments ago. She stood and went to look out the door, finding herself in a hallway, probably to the other bedrooms. From the hall window, she saw she was still on the second floor, and now had a view of the front approach to the house, and an impressive one it was. A road wide enough for two carriages paved with light-colored brick contrasted with the green lawn and low stone walls bordering the park. A courtyard directly in front of the house housed several statues and outbuildings for horses and other storage. The sun was beating down on it all with an uncharacteristic brightness.

Margaret Pinard

She became aware of the voices that could be heard from down the stairs and approached the banister to peer down.

Chapter 4

"I have absolutely no idea how she came to be here," Henry was saying, "but I intend to find out by questioning each of the staff personally. You may be present if you wish, for if there is going to be—" Henry broke off as he saw the pale young woman making her way down from the landing to the salon where he was speaking to the constable.

He paused and sought her eye, wondering if she had remembered who she was after the brief rest, or if instead she had forgotten again where she was. Concluding from her expression that neither of these was the case, he merely nodded politely to her and finished his sentence.

"If there is going to be an investigation, we of course support every effort of the police to find out what has happened and make it right, to our utmost ability." Henry felt the people of the room examining him at that moment; he was highly uncomfortable but tried to appear calm and in control. He met the young woman's eyes again. Indeed, he felt they had not left him since she started down the stairs. In spite of all the wild and whirling thoughts that had circulated in his brain in the past couple of hours—the shock of seeing the girl in his rooms in that state, the danger of scandal, the responsibility of protecting his family's reputation, the need for speedy disassociation with this mystery person—he felt as though he wanted to help her find her identity and shepherd her back to life.

If only Horace had not already called attention to the family in the neighborhood by being such a drunken idiot, I might do it, Henry thought.

The policemen turned and observed the woman descending, standing to greet her. Henry introduced Sergeant Ragby and Constable Norris to the young woman, who nodded politely but did not reveal any of her thoughts.

Norris asked, "Is there a room where we can ask a few questions privately, sir? While the sergeant is figuring out where to house her temporarily, of course."

"Yes, the library is right through this hallway to the left. It is at your disposal. Let one of the servants know if you require anything."

"Yes, thank you, sir. After you, ma'am, if you please."

As they proceeded down the hallway, Henry watched their backs with a wash of feelings fighting for mastery in his chest, protectiveness vying with fear and worry.

* * *

While the owner of the house spoke with the police sergeant, she was facing the constable, a middle-aged, ruddy-faced, country-looking sort who was feeling somewhat abashed at not only having to ask delicate questions of a woman, but also not knowing what her name or situation was. She appreciated his care; in his position, she would not know how to act properly either. She tried to make him at ease by being as direct and honest as she could.

"Constable, I wish I could be of more use in your investigation into what has happened but unfortunately, I have not yet recovered any personal memories before finding myself here. I do seem to know, that is, I presume that I am from a respectable position in polite society somewhere, since I am not at a loss for manners and understand how to manage servants. I'm not sure what that means…"

She lapsed into some inner thoughts on what it might mean. Constable Norris cleared his throat.

"Yes, Miss Alice—er, may I call you that, for the time being? I understand from Mr. MacFarlane you indicated that might be your name?"

"Yes, sir."

"Then, Miss Alice, we can go through the things you do remember, and perhaps draw some conclusions from that. But first, shall we not send in the doctor? He is waiting in the house. Are you hurt anywhere that needs seeing to?"

She shook her head but submitted to a cursory examination by the doctor who had been called. As he checked her eyes, ears, and elbows where she had been tied, she did an internal check. Her own assessment found no pain other than stiffness in her arms from the binding, which was quite minor. She could not tell how long she had been under the sway of another's power, but she felt that doubtless was what must have happened. She was thankful that she felt in good health but disconcerted by her body's toggling between unnatural levels of calm dullness and sharpened senses.

The conversation proceeded through things she did and did not know: china patterns, no; family crests, no; tea-pouring, yes; quality of woolens, yes; coal mine names, yes; ferry patterns to the Continent, yes; overland transportation companies, no. It went on and on, with Norris jotting down each yes or no and inventing categories as he thought of them. This process had continued for what seemed like several hours, when there was a light knock at the door to the library. A servant entered and asked if they needed refreshments to be served, as it was near noon.

"Yes, that is most obliging of Mr. McFarlane. Tell him thank you, and that a luncheon would be most welcome, right, miss?"

"Yes, I believe I am feeling in need of some sustenance," Alice said. "Do tell Mr. McFarlane I thank him for his pains."

The food came in, and the questioning continued.

Cooking of fish, yes; knowledge of French, no; knife skills, yes.

Plaid tartans, yes; face creams, no; piano, yes; saints' names, yes.

Germanic languages, no; knowledge of spirits, yes; European geography, very little.

Spiritualism. Yes.

Chapter 5

As Constable Norris was gazing at young Miss Alice speculatively, another knock came on the door.

"Please come in, the things are ready—ah, Sergeant! Yes, sir, apologies, sir. Have you had any news?"

The police sergeant stepped in and Alice felt nonplussed at the sight of the mid-sized man with a prominent belly not quite reined in by the policeman's belt. He was of average complexion with bleary-looking blue eyes that seemed to dart around, taking everything in.

"Well, then, miss," the sergeant said, "we have found a place for you to stay while you recover your memory and your health after this bit of a shock, although you do not look too ill-at-ease, which is a good sign." Sergeant Ragby observed the girl and waited for her to respond. Alice indeed felt ill-at-ease at his brusqueness but answered to satisfy him.

"Yes, Sergeant, in fact, I feel healthy in body, but I worry that not knowing my identity will worry me in spirit, so I have been trying as best I could to narrow down where I am from with your able constable here. And I should clarify that I feel a familiarity with the name Alice, as if it is important, but I am not certain it is my own name. I do not want to misdirect your search."

Circumspect, thought Ragby to himself. "Capital," he said out loud, "that is the type of specificity with which we can work and get some results. I hope for your sake they come soon, miss, to relieve your mind. We shall do our best." A slight pause, then, "We are monitoring Mr. McFarlane and his household due to the fact that they found you here, and that indicates some connection. You haven't managed to discover the connection there, have you?" His hopeful look to Norris was answered by a shaking of his head.

"Well, then, miss" he said again, this time to conclude, "I shall ask Norris to take you in the carriage to your temporary quarters at a nearby rectory. Do you require anything else before I continue with my inquiries here?"

"Yes, I would like to speak with Mr. McFarlane, please. And thank you for finding me a place. I appreciate the requests you have made on my behalf."

"You are most welcome, miss," said the

sergeant.

Norris led the way out to the hallway, Alice followed, and the sergeant took up the rear as they all went to meet the master of the house.

* * *

Having been evicted from his library, Henry was going over estate accounts, his chore whenever he was at home, in the salon. A small secretary was there for his sister's writing when she visited, and he had commandeered it for the day. In fact, though, he was not going over accounts very effectively, as his thoughts wandered constantly to the how, the why, and the what of the mystery unfolding in his own house.

As the police tramped through the hallway back to the salon, he closed the account book and stood, anxious to know whether anything had been discovered yet. The look on Sergeant Ragby's face revealed nothing, but the constable appeared confused as he looked over a list on his pad of paper.

"Well, gentlemen," Henry said, "if you need anything else from me or the household today, we are ready."

"Sir, we do. We shall go through with interviewing each of your staff, and I'll be the one to do it, so that Norris can transport the miss to her temporary quarters," said the sergeant.

"I did want to speak with you a moment before I go, Mr. MacFarlane, if I could," said the woman firmly, looking at Henry and not at the police.

"Of course."

* * *

The police stepped outside the salon, and Henry closed the pocket doors. They sat in the chairs by the fireplace, and he held his breath, waiting.

She was gazing mutely at the closed doors in a way that meant she also knew the police would be listening, he thought.

"I'd like to thank you sincerely for your reception of me," she said. Then she paused and made a motion with her hands that looked like writing with a pen. He understood and showed her to the desk where there was a stack of thick stationer's paper and a well-used fountain pen. She immediately strode over, speaking again.

"I still can't remember my life before—before today, but I hope that I will be able to put together the pieces of—of something, and become a useful human being again. The police—" she paused in her speech and in her writing. A few more fierce scribbles, then she eased the piece of paper under a folder and turned to face him. "The police will no doubt be able to do a better job of it than I will do, so I am off."

She offered her hand. He took it and said, "I have done nothing but what decency requires, but if

I can ever do more, do not hesitate to call on me."

He opened the door for her, and she didn't look back as she exited, followed by the police constable. He wasn't sure when he would see her again, and he was filled once more with fierce contradictory wishes.

Henry very much wanted to go straight to the paper to see what message she had left for him but he was afraid to see what it might reveal about the young woman—or indeed, about his family's involvement with her.

With a staff of twelve at the grand house, the police interviews lasted all afternoon, and Henry was unable to return either to his accounts or to the note she'd left. He did make sure to attend each servant's interview, little to the liking of the police sergeant. He argued for it based on the fact that he had better know what was going on in his own household, and the sergeant did not wish to contravene him, Mr. MacFarlane being a respected member of the community.

The young woman, who had realized that her name was not Alice, was in a carriage being secreted away by the police, her thoughts still at the grand house of Atwell. She was hoping very desperately that her new realization was accurate, and that what she had conveyed in her message would be enough to secure Henry MacFarlane as an ally.

Chapter 6

"Mr. MacFarlane, please be so good as to answer my rather impertinent question," Horace said in a mock stern voice, a twinkle in his eye.

"Horace, while I appreciate your attempts to distract me, I will not forget that we are meeting this morning to see what can be done about the problems you've created up and down the neighborhood by your behavior," Henry said sourly. "It is not something I relish talking of either, you know," he added.

"Right: younger brother is a success with the ladies, a whirlwind genius at the gaming tables—what is there to relish in that for you? Really, there is no need to stay jealous. You could do just as well if you put in the effort."

"Horace, how were you brought up so differently as to have such a different moral scale from the rest of us? I don't understand; it is simply not acceptable to engage a young woman's attentions with no intention of marrying her. You degrade her reputation, bad enough, but you also give your own family a bad name as well. We are in a business where honor and loyalty count for a lot, you know—"

"And I am not allowed to work in it beyond doing what you tell me," Horace interrupted. "It is hardly fitting work for someone like me, Henry. I need challenges. You know my school history; you know that."

There was a lull in the conversation as Henry contemplated his brother, six years his junior. "Can I trust you with something very volatile, something very discreet? I may regret it, but I think its importance would give you some gravity as well as a challenge for your mind."

Henry noted the perked ears and the immediate attention, heading it off with "But first, you must apologize to Mrs. Granthorpe and her daughter, and tell Lord Taylor that Anne Metcalfe is a charming young woman but you could never hope to keep her in the style she deserves, and so have enjoyed her company socially but have not dared to hope further. Does that accord with your wishes?" he asked.

"Fine, fine, it is what I would have had to do before my next project anyway, but yes, I will do that. But what is this challenge you are talking about? It does intrigue me."

Henry looked hard at his brother and pinned

him with a stare. "It involves someone's life in the balance, so if you can manage to be serious, it would be much more appropriate."

"All right, all right, serious, prepared, long face on. Is it to do with the money Father made on that last deal before he died?"

Henry continued his hard look. "No, but what do you know about that? Anything that could help us get the money back from that widow?"

"Not exactly that... just something in the papers that Father left me in his will. I started going through some of them a few months ago out of boredom, and they contain some very puzzling transactions. Perhaps you could study those, while I work on your problem, which must be..."

"Don't try to guess, Horace. And yes, it involves that woman."

* * *

A few minutes later found the brothers installed in the salon, where Henry pulled out the mysterious, maddening note.

I believe you are an ally. I do not know about the police. They are putting me in a rectory for recovery. Please visit when you can. I think Alice was my mother's name, but I know of no one else yet.

Horace read it several times, concentrating

on the tone, the information, the frantic sloped writing. He looked up at Henry to ask, "And you did not show this to the police a week ago?"

"No. I do not know Sergeant Ragby and did not know where this would put us in the eyes of the police, especially after your affairs and your debts."

Horace was about to say something, ground his mouth closed, then opened it again. "Wise, I would say, under the circumstances. I had nothing to tell them when they asked me about the whole affair. So have you been to see her? The girl not named Alice?"

"No."

"Also wise. Do you know which rectory? I imagine you've discreetly found out?"

"No, but I thought you might be able to do so, as you more regularly appear at the county churches…" Henry sighed. "For your own reasons, no doubt."

"Yes, well, I will keep straight as long as I have an active occupation. This will no doubt require all my skills. And for a noble cause! Or at least it seems so at first blush. I will do the best I can, with utmost discretion. Don't worry, Henry, or at least don't look so worried!" Horace laughed.

Chapter 7

That afternoon, the young lady in question was in the flower garden of the St. Agnes Rectory, on her knees cutting flowers for the church decorations, as the coming service would be for Easter. She liked doing it, as she could recognize and remember the names of most of the flowers as she cut them in turn, which pleased and encouraged her. She was in need of encouragement after a particularly hard interview with the Reverend Alexander LeFebre, her host, and a doctor he had procured to test her mental faculties.

A bleeding farce of a doctor, that buggering —how on earth—I wish I didn't know that kind of language, she thought, discontent again. This must be quite the untouched country parish indeed if his idea of mental faculty was to say your letters backwards and balance on one foot. My goodness! She picked up her skirts, one of several donations from the rector's wife, and shifted along the row of blooming flowers.

Delphinium, very pretty, she thought to herself. But not gaudy enough for the service as Mrs. LeFebre would like, of course. I wonder why she bothers to grow them if she only wants the lilies and roses. She sighed. She was trying to keep her note to Mr. MacFarlane out of her mind, but it kept sneaking back. She had had a strong feeling of confidence in him at the time, less in herself, and practically none in the police. That was over a week ago now, and he had not visited.

Since then, however, the police had been more than civil, appeared to take her side quite strongly, and were trying laboriously both to discover her identity and to find out how she had come to be here in Carknocke County near the east coast of England. So far she had remembered only her mother's name, which she had not divulged to the police. It would not have helped much with their search and she held onto it as an inner hope that other memories would return.

Mr. MacFarlane had not been heard from, heard of, or mentioned to her by anyone.

For want of a real name, she decided to take the name of the church's patron saint, Agnes. It would only be temporary. The rector LeFebre, and his wife took to it easily, and she now turned her head when the name 'Agnes' was mentioned.

She meditated on her family background and in what sort of circumstances her family may have been. She couldn't decide whether her family had been poor or not. The skills that the constable had asked her about seemed to point both ways, perhaps more on the poor side. She pondered the skills in the kitchen in which she had felt some confidence: tea service, cooking fish, knife skills, use of spirits. She got a twinge there that made her think of her father. God, she hoped he was not a drunkard.

Then her thoughts turned to the events of the morning. That silly Dr. Fenton had been ordering her into different positions, making her concentrate on her balance and throw dignity out the window. He was a doctor, though; there was a hope he would not gossip about his patients…

"No, there isn't," she said aloud, annoyed again at the rector's choice of a practitioner.

"What is that, Agnes? I didn't think you knew I was here. I was trying to be quiet." Agnes turned to see Mrs. Lefebre on a shaded seat at the edge of the garden row.

No doubt, so you could spy on me, thought Agnes, but said, "And you were, madam, I was just naming the flowers as I remembered them," she supplied easily. "You have some lovely spring blooms, I must say."

"Yes, you know most were planted by my antecedent here. The last vicar's wife had quite a hand for it. Me, I'm lucky they just keep coming up," Mrs. Lefebre pronounced contentedly. "Although I could wish for some grander flowers for an Easter service, I do know we have not the grand church for it. Ah, so it may be God has the glory instead, that is all well."

There was a pause as Agnes waited to see if she would say more, but evidently the missus just desired to sit and enjoy the warm air of the garden. Agnes moved the cutting basket yet again to the side and made to shift her skirts over and move herself when Mrs. Lefebre recommenced.

"I should tell you that you are welcome to attend the Easter service, Agnes. I know last Sunday you were not feeling up to it, but it would be good to hear about the Lord's resurrection while you are waiting for your own deliverance, whatever it may be. Most of the families in the country around come here. Only a few go to St. Giles, as it is not very convenient for carriages when it has been raining."

Agnes demurred, letting the rector's wife prate on, guarding her inner thoughts for later.

* * *

Easter came, and with it, a new overskirt and bonnet from Mrs. Lefebre. Agnes did not much care to examine herself in it, as she knew she looked pale and drawn from not sleeping well and working herself too hard, even if it was outside in the kitchen and flower gardens. She slipped her feet into the old servant's shoes she'd been given at Atwell weeks ago and wondered what the service would be like. Would it jar her memories loose and she would discover she was a minister's daughter herself? Would it jar her nerves, and all the people merely intimidate her? Or would it do nothing, and merely show to the whole community that she was a misplaced wanderer whom they did not know how to dispose of? She suspected the last option was the most likely.

She reviewed again the answers she had given to Constable Norris on religious matters: she knew saints' names and she knew about the Spiritualism Movement. In which direction did her family's practice tend? Knowing the saints' histories suggested Catholicism, as almost all Protestant churches now considered saints a tool of the papists. But the Spiritualists were an entirely different breed, given to showy demonstrations with spirits talking through people and nonsense of that kind. She'd heard of such things somewhere before. Agnes wished sorely for a mother to tell her what she wanted to know.

Mr. Lefebre and his curate, Mr. Dixon, were in front of the rood screen; the former intoning clear, strong words of wisdom while the latter stared determinedly downward at his clasped hands. Nothing had shocked her into remembering, yet nothing had seemed new or unfamiliar, either.

She was seated in the front row with the rector's small family, and therefore unable to scan the crowd for interesting features of faces, but she had the feeling they were all glancing over at her, wondering about her story. They no doubt were, since the mystery was probably the most exciting thing to happen in neighboring Goole-town in many a year, she thought unhappily. Agnes wished she were no longer there and no longer Agnes.

At the end of the service was a celebration with tarts and pies brought by the parishioners, which Agnes was going to decline politely, when she saw a face that jolted her. The man was chatting to a dark-haired young woman and obviously enjoying himself when he looked up and caught her eye. Her heart stopped. He was… familiar.

Horace looked at the young woman who had been seated with the rector's family and realized that his appearance produced a shock in her. Very well, he thought to himself, let us see how much damage we must undo here. He excused himself from the conversation with the lovely Lucy McBride and made his way unhurriedly through a few knots of people to present himself to Mrs. Lefebre and her "Agnes."

"How splendid you look, Mrs. Lefebre, and what a marvelous sermon your husband gave today. I was quite reformed by his tract on faithfulness and devotion, I must say."

"Oh, Mr. MacFarlane, how you flatter. And judging by your second statement being highly unlikely, we should deduce that the first, pertaining to me, is also unlikely?" she said, teasing as only a matronly middle-aged woman can do.

"No, most certainly not, madam. You appear to marvelous advantage in purple, as I believe I have told you before."

"Oh come, come, next you'll have me dressing just to please your eyes, even though they are seldom seen here in our parish. What have you to say to that?"

"I see that I have a worthy foe in wit and can do no more. Would it please you to introduce me to the young lady with you?" Horace said, turning toward Agnes, whose face still held the frozen look of confusion.

Mrs. Lefebre brushed a glance over Agnes and turned to Horace. "Mr. McFarlane, may I present Miss Agnes, who will be staying with us for a time while she recovers from a dreadful shock. Agnes," she turned to her, "this is Mr. Horace McFarlane, who lives a few miles north of us here at the parish. His family is one of the first in the county." Here she swept her gaze back to Horace, "although not always in attendance at our Sunday services, unfortunately for us."

Agnes was recovering from the reeling semi-recognition of his face and noting to herself the flirtatious tone of Mrs. Lefebre toward this man. She was wondering how he fit into her own puzzle, when he addressed her directly.

"Miss Agnes, I must admit I am seldom here on Sundays, but I may plead duties of the household to attend to, which often take me as far away as Newcastle or Glasgow. I might even dare to suggest that you might on occasion have similar duties that require your attention on a Sunday," he said amiably.

"I do try to come to the service whenever I can, sir. I have always felt at home in the Church."

"Really? Well, that is a credit to you and to the good minister's wife, I am sure," at which remark Mrs. Lefebre preened a bit more. "Have you ever been to a big city, a city of industry and trade such as Newcastle? They can be terribly noisy and unpleasant, but as I said, if one has to go, one has." He winked at Mrs. Lefebre as he said, "I do try to be as obliging as possible to matters regarding my family's business interests, even though it is my brother at the helm and I am supposedly free to pursue other things. But come, have you been? It can be quite diverting."

Agnes was not sure why he was asking her such leading questions but confined her answers strictly to generalities. "No, I'm afraid not, sir. I should think that the commotion would not be good for me while I am recovering."

"No, of course you are right. I see you've a good practical head on your shoulders. Perfectly sensible. Better to take your ease in the country for a bit, have the good missus look after you and then return to your people when you are much stronger. Where will you be headed when you return, if I might ask? I thought I—"

Mrs. Lefebre interrupted, looking a little agitated at the line of questioning as well. "I don't know what this talk of cities and country is for, but I can assure you, Mr. McFarlane, we are taking very good care of Miss Agnes and expect her to make a full recovery come summer." She put a small hand on Agnes' back to steer her away, turning to Horace to say, "I believe my husband may want to talk to you, sir, back in the church. Farewell and Godspeed in your business, as always."

"Very nice to meet you, sir," said Agnes, before being steered into the lane going to the house.

Horace didn't respond audibly but bowed graciously as the two women walked away. He had not gotten very far with his impertinent questions, but it had been worth a try. He kept his eye on the smaller retreating figure, turning over in his mind what he had seen and heard.

Chapter 8

Sergeant Ragby was pacing the carpet on the floor of his personal study, his rich walnut desk awash in piles of paper, and his assistant, Barton, seated near the door but following his progress with a nervous eye. He had seen his sergeant in a state like this several times before, and it usually resolved itself in a case well closed, but this stage was always a bit treacherous to navigate.

"So you said," Barton began, "that no one had anything to say to the photograph? Neither at the rail station nor at the river docks." A pause. "But that you think her accent is put on—a better class than she is, say?" Another pause, but no interruption to the pacing. "Hmmm," intoned Barton, hoping this would be enough to start Ragby talking.

It wasn't.

"And the staff of the household do not seem to have had anything to contribute. Nothing seen going in or out that morning, no deliveries, no messages." Here Barton paused again, tired of this game. "There is that new servant though, that—"

"Yes, I know, Gerard. Thinking on him. No connections, though." Ragby grunted tersely.

"Have you asked his employers about his references yet? I believe he came from the north. Or are you still worried about them, the MacFarlanes?"

"Still worried. Worried, indeed," was all Ragby would say. Barton wondered if the sergeant's interview with Horace had contributed to his worry. He did have the reputation of being a flirt, but nothing so bad as kidnapping. Besides, if a servant had found the girl tied up like that, it would have been all over the village and across the fields to Leeds, where the bulk of their business was done. That would be shooting themselves in the foot, he would say.

As it was, the manservant Arthur was trusted as a member of the family and no one else had seen her condition when found, it seemed. No doubt it might have been easier if they could interview the villagers too but in the interest of discretion, they were only pursuing professional channels.

"Well, at least Dr. Fenton came back with good news," Barton said. "She won't be disappearing on us; she seems rather determined to get to the bottom of this herself, from what I heard from Constable Norris. Have you had the doctor's report?" asked Barton.

Another minute went by before Sergeant Ragby looked up from his measured pacing, saying, "The doctor, yes. She does not appear to be at risk of running away, and neither does she seem troubled in the mind. But I think we will need another kind of doctor to determine what else happened to her, and her whole history."

Ragby paused. "What do you think the girl would say to a hypnotist?"

Chapter 9

"It's not that I don't feel a sense of responsibility, Henry, of course I do! I just know that I have different skills than you. I have to work out my own way of helping the business. I can't do it your way, because you're the director and because I just can't!" Horace finished with a plaintive look at his brother, who sighed.

"I know you've struggled, Horace. I hope I've helped you sort out some of that. I think we're in a stage here where things are evolving, changing, and I'm not sure which way to go, which is why," he broke off after seeing Horace's surprised look. "Yes, it is true, I do not know everything in the world, which is why I need your help on this matter before you go back to supervising the mines."

There was a lull in the energy of the small room where they talked: their thoughts turned to the western coal towns, the landscape of the mines, the death, the politics, all that contributed to their wealth, and all that their father had anticipated doing to better the situation of those living there in the towns that served the Selby-McFarlane lines.

Henry sighed. "If our father were alive, what would he do about finding her here? Would he know where she had come from? Who dropped her here to drag our name through the mud? At least the police have kept her manner of discovery quiet, but there are still no answers, and I need answers if we are to stay safe here. I wish very much she would simply tell us, but from what you say, she still has no memory, and from what the police have told us, I believe we are still suspect and thus cannot merely pay her a visit to talk." He sighed again, feeling defeated.

"I need help from your other sources, Horace. I'm sorry to have to ask, but we truly need the help."

"All right. I'll leave for the north tonight to find out what I can from the rail contacts," Horace said. "You'll let me know by telegram if the police come up with anything?"

"Of course."

Chapter 10

Agnes' desire to discover her family background had sent her to the nearest library, at Ferningham Manor, where the family in residence kept a full-volume set of the history of the great families in England. She had already come three times to see if any of the names stirred a particular, strong feeling of connection, but so far nothing had rung true, and she had got all the way to the letter 'S.'

This afternoon the lady of the house was in but unoccupied, so she had settled in to share the library with this strange new woman in the neighborhood, about whom not much was known. To Agnes' vexation, Lady Alslip was attempting to glean some information from her, which she could have the pleasure of sharing at her next social visit.

"Do you know, I have distant family that descend from the Angleseys of Portsmouth," Lady Alslip said.

"I hear they are a very fine family," Agnes dutifully replied, even though she'd heard nothing

of the sort. She knew the sort of woman Lady Alslip was, perfectly graceful in company, but always
scheming to be one-up among her social set. She
saw through the cozy restfulness to the fretful cam-
paigner below. She wondered if she'd always had
this gift of perception. She wished it would bring
her memory back more quickly.

"Yes, have you been to Portsmouth? It is
such a fine town, and if one has occasion to rest
there, one would not regret the fortification it pro-
vides for the harried life of running a household."

Ah, so you are trying to determine whether I
run a household, thought Agnes. "I have not had
occasion to visit Portsmouth, as far as I can remember, but I hope to one day." There, leave her with
that, she thought. If she recognized the social lady's
type so easily, could it be because she had had
many examples of it in her former life? The further
she thought, the more sense this made to her, but
she was getting no further with her name search, so
she politely drew the visit to a close, hoping that on
the next visit Lady Alslip might be otherwise engaged.

Chapter 11

It was a warm late spring day, and Agnes was walking slowly and keeping to the shade in order not to arrive in disarray at the rectory, where comments would be made. Lady Alslip's estate was two miles from the rectory grounds, and she was just coming round the low hill where the rectory appeared to come from nowhere—she liked that viewing experience—when she took a final rest on the grass, prolonging her time out-of-doors and out of earshot.

Several weeks had passed and the duration of uncertainty was starting to wear down Agnes' spirit and resolve. I will not fall into destitution. I am from a good family, she repeated to herself, somewhere. If only I knew where to turn next.

With that attempt at fortification but with a still-brooding heart, she rose and walked slowly to the Lefebres' door.

Upon entering, she heard voices in the parlor, and hoped she could avoid showing herself there by dashing across the hallway silently. She did not get the chance however, since Mrs. Lefebre's maid had been posted to wait for her return. The visitor was a Mr. McFarlane to see her, and he and the missus had been talking for a quarter of an hour while waiting for her, she was informed.

Mentally girding herself against showing the same reaction she had at church last week, she entered the room and showed a different reaction entirely; it was not Mr. Horace McFarlane, but Mr. Henry who had come to call.

He rose to greet her, with a kind politeness, and they settled down after allowing Mrs. Lefebre to introduce them. The woman knew that Agnes had been 'found' near the McFarlane estate; Agnes was very grateful at this moment that more particulars had not been divulged.

"Good afternoon, sir, thank you for your visit. I'm sure you have far greater things to think about, even on a Saturday, so it is most kind of you," said Agnes.

"Indeed there are many items of business to attend to, even on a Saturday, but I could not pass another day without coming to see how you were faring. Of course, you are being taken care of by the best people possible," with a glance and nod at Mrs. Lefebre, who murmured her half-hearted disavowal, "but I hope to hear you have had some discoveries or news that have pierced the mystery of your situation. It very much troubles me," he said, with a rather distressed look.

"No more troubling to you, sir, I hope, than it is to me," Agnes returned, resentment flaring at his words. "In fact, the police make very little progress in discovering more about the circumstances, and I have not had my memories return, either recent ones or very old ones. One of the detectives said it might be one or the other at first, as has happened in other cases of amnesia, but I have had neither. I continue to rely on the powers of observation and ... and a sense of familiarity, when it comes."

"Do you mean that you recognize certain places, names, faces? That should definitely help the police, should it not?" Henry asked. Of course his brother had told him of her reaction at church.

"No, not exactly those things," she said, ignoring his veiled reference. "For instance, I was out cutting flowers for the Easter church service—"

"And a beautiful job you did with my flowers, Agnes—I heard so many compliments on the arrangements!" Mrs. Lefebre interrupted.

"Thank you, ma'am," she said, turning her gaze back to Mr. McFarlane. "The flowers. I knew all their names, and more, as if I was used to arranging them, or seeing them, or had studied them, or something. I know it doesn't seem like much, but that is the sort of information I am trying to piece together. I have not come to any conclusions yet, sir," she added, watching his eyes come back to focus on the scene in the parlor from wherever they had been cast internally. Could she really trust this Henry MacFarlane, who now seemed so distant, so caught up in his own affairs?

"I'm sorry to hear that things are coming so slowly, Miss—Agnes," he paused, wrinkling his brow and looking down. "I would offer my assistance, but I've no idea—"

"Of course you've no idea how to help," Agnes interrupted. "Neither do I. Neither do the police." She felt suddenly impatient with the polite niceties being uttered, as her frustration with her own ignorance bubbled up.

"Mr. and Mrs. Lefebre here are very kind to me, but I realize that even if I do not discover my memory, soon I must change my situation. I cannot rely on your generosity forever, Mrs. Lefebre," she said, and turned back to Mr. McFarlane. "Thank you for your effort in coming to see us here, Mr. McFarlane. I know it can be no small distance."

"Oh, but of course you'll stay for tea, sir," Mrs. Lefebre cajoled. "Do tell us what your family is doing these days. One cannot trust Mr. Horace's reports half the time!"

Henry capitulated, staying for tea, being pleasant but much more reserved in manner than his brother had been to the lady of the house. An awkwardness between Agnes and him remained, as she felt he had reneged on his offer of help, and he felt she had rebuked him for being insensitive. Their conversation maintained a strained politeness.

Chapter 12

It had taken no small feat of discreet enquiries, a discipline in which Constable Norris did
not excel, to decide at last on the right hypnotist for
the job. He had started asking the country doctors,
but they had only mistrust and disapproval of the
new quackery. Then he had asked the professors at
the local medical school, and one had given him
three names. Only one of those had responded to
his repeated calling cards, and he seemed more of a
fake than someone who truly knew the science end
of the craft. He had, however, let slip the name of
an envied rival, and it was this man, a Mr. Tunbridge, on whom the constable had settled for an
interview. He had met with the doctor briefly,
enough to see a good-fitting suit, hear a staid accent, feel comforted by the rhythm of unfamiliar
but medical-sounding jargon, and have a spot of
tea. Now he was to communicate all this to the
sergeant, and quite proud of his work he was.

"Come," said the sergeant from behind his

study door.

Norris entered and half-bowed to his superior officer before seating himself to make his report. Ragby looked tired but satisfied. In a similar style to his terse musings with his assistant Barton, the report-out commenced.

* * *

Ragby: "Norris, good of you to come out here to the house. I do hate driving down to town when it is so pleasant out here. Now, I think we're ready to move on this case of the girl up at Tidewater."

Norris: "Yes, sir. I—"

Ragby: "I spoke with my clerk, Barton—you know him? No matter, he recommended a specialist in this hypnotism quackery, a Dr. Tunbridge from down at the University in Grantham. Have you heard of him?"

Norris: "Yes, sir, in fact—"

Ragby: "Really, Norris! I didn't know you went in for that sort of thing. I had thought it would be quite the thing for the young people, but not for us more sensible and law-abiding folk. Well, perhaps there is something real in it after all. But there's no need for you to worry about it any more than necessary; I think we've rather exhausted you on this case, and it is high time I let you return to your regular duties. You've been an immense help, Constable Norris, in this affair, as I know I can trust your discretion in dealing with the gentlefolk."

Norris: "Thank you, sir. I—"

Ragby: "No, no trouble at all. I'll have some commendation or other for you at the next policemen's dinner, how's that? Now, do make yourself acquainted with Barton, he's my new right-hand man on this case and may need a little local knowledge. There's a good chap."

Norris, with a sigh: "Yes, sir. Good day, sir."

Chapter 13

On her last trip to Lady Alslip's estate, Agnes had finished her run through the names in the last volume of England's great families. Nothing had stirred her mind as a familiar association might have, so she was resigned to thinking of her family background as that of a poor, nameless tribe. She hoped that at least they were decent folk.

Agnes sat on an embroidery chair in the Lefebres' living room, repairing the edges of the linen napkins that been waiting for a more expert hand than that of the day-maid. She found she could easily hook the stitches back into place, minute as the loops were. As she hooked and pulled, twisted and tightened with her needle, she lost the tense agitation of doubting her every move and action. Things seemed to calm down, and the voices trying to pierce the mystery in which she was engulfed were stilled. She worked on until she came to the end of the pile, undisturbed. As she folded each napkin over and piled them neatly together, Agnes felt a surge of pride and turned to present the pile to someone—but to whom?

She felt like a schoolchild who had completed an assignment, correctly and ahead of time, and was waiting to be patted on the head. Whence came this feeling? Had she worked as a seamstress, a lace-worker? No, there was something warmer about the pride she felt; she'd been taught how to sew by her mother. Mother. A warm glow surrounded her but then immediately departed.

Agnes wished for more—a glimpse of her mother's face as she sat by her knee, the touch of her hand as she put her to bed, but there was nothing. Just that warm rush of pride after repairing a pile of linens. A sob contracted her chest, and she left the ivory-colored linens on the seat, retreating to her narrow room where she tried to calm herself and put the unknown past out of her mind.

Chapter 14

Horace had been through Leeds and York on his family's private rail car and talked with all the deputy station managers he knew. Usually he was extracting information about competitors' loads of stock going through, treading the fine line between being the grand gentleman providing drink and the worthy confidant of trade talk. Horace had become very good in the past few years at balancing these two roles people needed him to play in order to let go of their valuable insider information.

He was currently on his third city in the search for information about the girl now known as Agnes, and very little had turned up. The police had finally given Henry a copy of the photograph, taken at the MacFarlanes' own house, and Horace was now showing it to their rail line employees to ask if they had seen her in the past few months.

The photograph had elicited a few raised eyebrows and low whistles, as the common man assumed he knew why Horace was asking: spurned lover, jealous rival, something along those lines. This bothered Horace but little; he was glad it spiced his enquiries with the need for secrecy. God knew, this had as much to do with his pride as their assumption would have it. Family reputation counted for something in his book, as much as that fact might surprise Henry.

Edinburgh was next for enquiries, and he didn't relish it. Horace turned from his desk where he was perusing his notes to get a drink from the cabinet. He had less and less hope the further he got from Carknocke County, since he believed Agnes was most likely from one of the surrounding counties, her accent and manners fitting in so naturally. Still, she was queer in some way... or perhaps that was the amnesia. Why had she reacted so strongly when she had seen him? That was what puzzled him.

Still, he could always combine the trip north with seeing to the jute mills, an irksome duty that could be checked off the list for the year. He'd had a letter from his brother Henry that related the disappearance of one of their servants, a manservant who'd been hired to replace Horace's aging valet when the time came. Henry had reported it to the police, with little hope in their being able to chase down the lead.

But at least the MacFarlanes knew that their staff could still be trusted. Small comfort.

Chapter 15

Agnes had come to her decision: after almost four months, she could no longer stay at St. Agnes, both for her sake and the Lefebres'. She had written Sergeant Ragby to ask what would be best in terms of her location for the investigation, indicating that she hoped to find work in Leeds, the nearest city at thirty miles' distance. Nothing further had come to her, and she wanted very much to get on with her life in a new situation if this was all she ever got back of her memory.

In response to her note, Sergeant Ragby had quickly replied he would come to call that day. Agnes was prepared to justify her decision to move, and was hoping that the sergeant might have found out more about her case through talks with the servants or other inquiries. She was happy that Mrs. Lefebre was out visiting parishioners for the afternoon and Mr. Lefebre was in his rectory office composing a sermon so they did not have to hear her argument for leaving.

When Sergeant Ragby arrived, the maid let him into the small parlor. He was followed by a middle-aged man, dressed in country tweed, and sporting a long, droopy mustache. "This is Dr. Tunbridge, Miss Alice—I mean, Agnes. Glad to hear you've been making some discoveries, well, at least one or two."

Dr. Tunbridge seemed to glance up at Agnes from his bushy eyebrows at this statement, but quickly blinked and returned his gaze to the sergeant. Agnes looked at him briefly and wondered why her note had been answered with such alacrity if they were just going to be trying her patience with another quack of a doctor, and not giving her any new information. Still, she would make it clear to Sergeant Ragby that her mind was made up.

"We have been hard at work as well. Dr. Tunbridge is here to examine your memory, and I'll be taking notes as you answer questions. Not to worry," he said, as she narrowed her eyes at the mention of her memory. "You'll get to see them, too. Doctor?" Ragby said, turning to the man.

Dr. Tunbridge appeared quite at ease, as if he were used to examining memories. This seemed peculiar to Agnes, but she was prepared to answer some questions before asking her own of the sergeant. She waited for the doctor to open up the interview, but he seemed loath to do so. She was on the verge of saying something when he looked up from his hands and met her gaze. His eyes boldly bored into hers, and she shrank back involuntarily, deciding to wait.

He asked her to close her eyes and concentrate on a memory, any memory. His eyes had great depths of blue, and she felt drawn to comply.

"Now think about this memory, who is in it, how it made you feel. Think about every detail, the light, the sound. Let's think about the sound and see if we can focus on that aspect. What sounds do you hear in the memory?"

Agnes listened as he spoke, trying to oblige, even though the memory she was using was only a few seconds old. She concentrated on the present sounds in the room: the mantel clock ticking, the birds calling outside, the faraway bleating of sheep in the fields. The clock was the nearest and loudest, and as she relaxed into the rhythm, everything else seemed to fade away.

"Now that sound," Dr. Tunbridge said quietly, "will keep going forever, so use it as your guide to your memories. You will not get lost. The sound is there to guide you," he almost whispered. The sergeant watched, so caught up himself that he was unable to take notes, as the girl's head dropped, tired, losing its own power, until she looked like a sleeping patient at the hospital, lacking her own volition. After a prolonged moment of this, he glanced at Dr. Tunbridge, who was staring keenly at the girl, watching for certain signs, Ragby supposed. After another moment, he spoke to her again, still quietly.

"Now that you are fully immersed in the memory of that sound, we will begin," and here, he looked at Sergeant Ragby to make sure his pencil was still in his hand. It wasn't.

"What is your name?" he asked.

"Euphemia May Broderick."

The men looked at each other, one shocked, the other calculating.

"Where are you from?" Dr. Tunbridge asked.

"Drogheda," she said with a perfectly British accent.

Sergeant Ragby looked even more amazed —his raised brows exclaimed "Ireland?!" but his mouth stayed closed. Dr. Tunbridge, though, was staying in for more, his brows fiercely knit and his mustachios fairly trembling with his concentration.

"Have you lived in Drogheda all your life?" he asked.

"No, my family moved to Glasgow when I was two years old. That is where I grew up."

"Why don't you have an Irish accent, or a Glaswegian one then?" asked Dr. Tunbridge.

"I do, but I was trained to speak like this."

"When? By whom?"

"When I—" here, she jerked sideways, knocking her head against the arm of the chair but showing no reaction. "When I left Glasgow. It was —" here she jerked again, her feet pushing against the floor and her body twisting up and over the seat. "I can't say whom," she said as she sagged against the base of the seat from the floor.

At this point, Sergeant Ragby was becoming worried for her safety, and the implications her replies had already pointed to—that she had been hypnotized and then trained for some nefarious purpose—would give them a square lead in the investigation. He squeezed the doctor's forearm, catching his attention, and gave him a look that said "wrap it up." As he did so, Agnes started screaming.

"I can't say! I can't say! I don't know him! I can't say—I won't say a thing, I promise!" Annie the maid came running in, startled by the screaming, then careening to a halt at the picture of the woman twisting on the floor, shouting in fear.

Ragby seized Tunbridge's arm. "Do something!" he shouted, and went to pick up Agnes, placing her on the chair to avoid further injury. As Ragby caught her wrists, she fought him, flailing her arms wide and screeching. He set her down and knelt in front of her, pinning her arms to the armrests of the chair, then turned to the doctor to say, "Well, take her out of it!"

Dr. Tunbridge came close to the pair of them then, and the sergeant and he could both see the tears streaming down her cheeks, though her expression again looked blank. The doctor turned to the maid and asked for a handkerchief. He used it to wipe her face, then spoke in a murmur.

"There, there, you don't have to say who it was, then, Euphemia." She jerked but was held in place by Ragby. "No need to say it if you can't. We'll help you say it when you're ready. For now, why don't you focus on that sound? It will always be there as your guide, remember."

The doctor turned to hand the handkerchief back and saw the Reverend Lefebre, standing stock-still in the doorway to the parlor, arrested by the sight of what he took to be an assault. Tunbridge held up one finger, as if to say "Wait" and continued.

"Now remember what was with the sound, in that one memory; there was light, there were people." Here he motioned Ragby to let go and stand back. He did, sitting back down in his own seat, and Tunbridge's soft voice continued. "There was a time and a place for that memory, so we are going to think about that. And maybe next time we'll be able to get at a different memory. You can open your eyes now."

Dr. Tunbridge's expression had gone from intense scrutiny back to a calm, still depth by the time Agnes opened her eyes and glanced around the room again, with Annie hovering and the Reverend Lefebre just behind, his mouth in a grim line.

"I don't think that was very helpful," Agnes said. "I don't have the right memories to bring back the past, since they are all recent. Good afternoon, Mr. Lefebre, I don't remember hearing you come in. Do you know Dr. Tunbridge? Sergeant Ragby has brought him today to help me examine my memory." Agnes' words tumbled over each other in a nervous gallop.

"I do not know him yet, but I would like to speak to both of you gentlemen in the study, if that's convenient," he said, not waiting for their acquiescence. They followed, and Agnes was alone again.

She stood and gingerly felt her head and her shoulder. She supposed the interview must have given her a headache, but what could have happened to her shoulder?

Chapter 16

Edinburgh's New Town was all right, Horace supposed, all clear lines and crisp corners of stone. But the Old Town of Edinburgh was where he was bound, around the rail yards and soot-blackened crumbling wrecks from earlier centuries, some that had been entirely swallowed by the ground. He was looking for a particular contact, if you could call him that: Mr. Carbrey Kincaid.

Kincaid was that type of man who knew everybody's business but made sure nobody knew his, which was generally blackmail or extortion or some other racket. He had been brought up roughly in the Old Town, one of its scrappy sons, and had an ear for overhearing and an eye for observing that made the use of his other facial features unnecessary. Thus, he went around town with a scowl and constantly spat in the street, the effect of a long tobacco habit.

Horace, fine gentleman that he was, had come to know Mr. Kincaid through the latter's attempt to blackmail him. It had backfired and Horace had forever after had a toehold over him, which he used to glean information that could help the family business. This time, he had to be very careful to make it sound like a business matter instead of what it was, a family scandal, to avoid a reversal of the toehold.

Kincaid turned his head to glare at Mr. McFarlane's fine top hat, and spat in the gutter of the alley where they were hovering, hidden from view by the McFarlane coach at the head of the alley.

"Crimes on the other rail lines, eh? Wha, so you can point to your own spotless record, is tha' it?" Spat again. "Course there're crimes. What kind you lookin' for?"

"The sensational kind. The kind that would have well-bred women and children taking our lines instead of Warburn's or Chatsworth's."

"A murder, like?"

"Yes, or a kidnapping or something. And if you've heard of one on our lines, we'll put it around that it was on theirs. Something recent, though, that has a victim that one could see in the press. So maybe not a murder. Solving a kidnapping would be better, eh?"

Kincaid eyed him hard, sensing an uneasiness but not knowing where it lay.

Spat again.

"A'right. I think I've got an idea, but I'll

need to talk round."

"Good," Horace spat out himself, stingingly aware of how fine an edge he was walking. "I'll be back day after tomorrow for particulars."

Chapter 17

With his brother dispatched to find some clues to the mystery, Henry MacFarlane was rather ill-at-ease to be sitting at home in the quiet mint-green parlor his mother had last had a hand in decorating some twenty years ago. He paced the room. He felt powerless to take any action that would not make his family's situation look worse.

'Can't travel, can't oversee, can't ask questions, damn!' he thought. He had had a report from the sergeant that they had found no firm leads, but were still trying to establish the girl's background and a possible motive, which might lead them to a perpetrator. Henry had been not a little alarmed at the sound of the letter he'd been sent. Ragby had reported that while Agnes would be moving out to the city to pursue gainful employment, having at least isolated certain facts with the help of the police (her name, her family history, etc.), the police would continue to investigate the situation and periodically check on her progress.

It was that phrase "with the help of the police" which had frightened Henry. He had had little helpful information from Horace and his northern contacts, and nothing of use from the police. They seemed to have left him alone, but he feared he was not yet clear of their suspicion. If the police were to know and control the whereabouts of the young lady, he would never be able to figure out the mystery, which made him feel unbearably vulnerable.

The shocking audacity of Agnes' arrival at Atwell made him more and more certain his family had been the target of someone's malicious intent. And Henry had no faith in the police to keep Agnes' discovery silent.

Arthur knocked and entered the parlor, carrying a letter on a tray for Henry. It was from the Reverend LeFebre. He unfolded the short message and read,

"Dear Sir,

After much hard thinking I have come to write to you of a certain delicate matter. In my wife's absence and mine, Sgt. Ragby saw fit to bring a practicer of hypnotism into my home to interrogate the young woman who goes by the name of Agnes. The visit quite terribly upset her, though she remembers nothing of it. I desire to speak to you of what transpired, since with this field I am quite unfamiliar. Your having first found the woman on your property and helped the police with the initial investigation, I thought you might be ready to assist again. I remain,

Your humble servant,

A. Lefebre"

Henry MacFarlane stared at the letter, now confirmed in his fears. The poor girl, he thought. What has she got in the middle of?

Henry now knew in which direction he and Horace must focus their enquiries: the new pseudo-science of 'Mesmerism.'

Chapter 18

"Able-bodied woman—" No, she did not want to emphasize that she would do physical work. It was a lady's maid she wished to be, not a chamber-maid.

"Able young woman—" Well, but was she sure of how old she was? Perhaps it did not matter, as long as she had a reference from Mrs. Lefebre.

"...Seeks employment as lady's maid. Can sew, embroider, arrange flowers." Now that didn't sound right. Ladies arranged flowers, not their maids, didn't they? But she also knew about cooking. What she felt in her fingers was such a puzzlement, Agnes almost despaired of finding her true identity, but she resolutely pushed that thought away and resolved yet again to create her own.

"I will not be fodder for the poorhouse; that is for certain." She finished writing her advertisement for the paper and sat at the desk for some moments, thinking of others to whom she could write. The list numbered exactly one: Henry Mac-

Farlane. But how did she feel about him, now that he had come and gone and seemed so caught up in his own affairs, even as he questioned her?

She supposed she must allow that he was in a fragile position as well, having discovered her and having such a strange mystery of a crime attached to his reputation, but still... her own life hanging in the balance should matter more than a reputation, should it not?

She did not feel up to writing him.

Instead, she told Mrs. Lefebre she would walk down the lane to the Morgans' house, two miles distant. Mr. Morgan played the organ for Rev. Lefebre's services, and had a pianoforte in his drawing room, a fact discovered by Agnes on her first visit there, several weeks before. Mr. Morgan's manner was more effusive than that of the reserved Lefebres, and he had encouraged her to sit and play it as she liked.

More visits had followed, as Agnes at first hesitantly, then with more confidence, allowed her fingers to do the playing instead of trying to remember the names of pieces to play. This time she did not find Mr. Morgan at home, but Mrs. Morgan received her and after a few moments of chatting, sat with her letters to distant family as Agnes softly played on the pianoforte.

Just like with the embroidering, there was something barely out of her reach as she played. It thrilled along her spine and tingled along her fingers as her hands kept time for a melody she did not remember, stroked keys whose sound she could somehow predict.

The light tinkling melody she played now drew to a close, and Mrs. Morgan smiled at her. "That was a lovely one, dear. What is its name?"

"I'm not sure," Agnes replied. "I learned many songs by repetition instead of reading the music, I'm afraid," she said, making up the excuse on the spot. As she said it, she wondered if it were true. She drew a piece of music-paper from the top of the instrument, looking at the bars, chords, sweeps, and strange symbols. She had no idea what they meant. So it was true, she had mimicked someone's playing to learn these, instead of learning how to read music.

"I will be leaving the neighborhood soon, Mrs. Morgan, but please thank your husband for allowing me the use of the piano for these past few weeks. It has been very good for my nerves. I thank you very much for your kind reception of me as well, ma'am," she finished, meaning it with all her heart.

Chapter 19

Horace drew up to the filthy wynd entrance in his carriage, with a heart that seemed to be bursting at his throat from the risk he was taking. He only hoped that the information Kincaid had gleaned contained nothing on his family and that he would not betray his feelings at the reception of the information. He was usually very adept at this, but he had recently received a telegram from Henry that contained some cause for alarm.

HYPNOTIZED STOP SEARCH FOR DOCTORS STOP RETURN QUICKLY STOP

His blood had run cold at the first word, as his mind jumped to his one brush with the 'science' of Mesmerism and whether the young woman had been involved in a similar type of knavery. He hoped not.

The unignorable spitting noise had commenced, so Horace knew it was time to alight and meet with Kincaid. Play the part, he told himself.

"What have you found?" he queried the shadowy shape at the end of the wynd, from a healthy distance.

"Nothing solid but a few that could be spun into a sugar-fancy, if ya like," came the reply. "Ther'as three girls that were reported missin' in the past several months and none of 'em turned up suicides. Ya go a bit further back though and there's a bit of other traffic," Kincaid said, a nasty smile on his face.

"Have you got names? Likenesses? It would help if it was a young beauty for the papers, you know."

"Oh, aye," said Kincaid. "I've made up a list of those missing, and the lines you could point 'em to, they're some of the Chatsworths', but it's not exactly—"

"Give it me." Horace scanned the scrawled list of a dozen names. None of them meant anything to him, but he looked at the train journeys they had taken and his eye stopped at one: Berwick. Where his own brush with the science had taken place.

Chapter 20

"We are ready to escort her to Leeds, sir, where she may be much less of a target, as being in the general mass of people. There would also be more men available on the Force to observe her comings and goings. I cannot but think that would be preferable to keeping her here in the county within the reach of suspect persons."

So said the visiting police constable who had come at Sergeant Ragby's request for this errand. He irked Ragby with his air of city superiority, but after the scene in the Lefebres' parlor, Ragby had had to take some decisive steps to allay the minister's concern. He had seen the man white with suppressed emotion in his study after the episode, staring at him and Dr. Tunbridge in turn, choosing his words with difficulty. If Ragby had known the effect a hypnotism would have on the girl, of course he would have been more circumspect about arranging the interview, but she had mentioned her intention to set out for the city, and he had felt that the hypnotist would give them some clues quickly. Well, and he had, at that.

Ragby sighed, and addressed his inferior, "Thank you for your readiness, Constable. While I couldn't say at present more on the suspect persons, I know you will appreciate the need for discretion in such a potentially volatile case. We will do our part to follow up on the information we obtained, and you and your colleagues will make sure to monitor the girl's movements and protect her as best you can from a distance. This is not a trap we set for her, of course. It's for her own good, but I do not think she would take kindly to feeling watched. The mind is surely a fragile thing once it is broken."

The city man nodded. "If I may ask, Sergeant, how is she to find employment when she don't know what 'er line of work is?"

"She is acting by instinct, Constable, and that will help us perhaps more than it will her."

Chapter 21

Henry's favorite hunter, a spirited bay named Herodotus, was doing the right thing not to listen to his rider's cues on this ride. Henry was much agitated, and the animal seemed to know he should ignore it, trotting evenly through the park and the woods to the east of the house. The rider's mind was churning between the Lefebre note, his brother's absence, and a recent visit from the police, after which he had had the clear impression he was now certainly considered suspect in the goings-on since the arrival of Alice—or Agnes—or whatever her name was. His mind was bouncing between seeing his family's downfall and ruin and imagining what could have happened to the girl and who could have done it. Such grim and grisly images floated through his head that he could feel himself sweating, his rattled nerves making him pale.

Once he left the park behind him, Henry urged the horse to a gallop. "Come, Roddy, no time to tarry," he said, flicking the crop to the horse's flanks.

* * *

Mr. Lefebre was at home this Saturday morning, having received Mr. MacFarlane's response to his note the day before. He awaited the arrival of the MacFarlane post-chaise, fairly pale himself, and overwrought with the events that had transpired around him.

Surely the police should have checked with me before putting Agnes through such an interview, he thought to himself. I would never have allowed it. Hypnotism indeed! More like mental torture of the soul, such things as God never condoned.

He looked up again through the curtains of his small parlor, thankful that his wife was still asleep and Agnes had not yet come down. Through the window, he saw MacFarlane on a horse, felt a momentary confusion, and then approved of the man's judgement in coming as discreetly as possible, without alerting more servants than necessary.

The rector went to meet him in front of the house, ushering him in and motioning for him to leave the horse's reins over the garden fence. As he did so he noticed a flash in the younger man's eyes and a stiff set to his jaw. His hair had become disheveled. They entered and sat in the parlor, not facing each other directly.

"Sir, I would not have dreamed of perturbing

you with something so below your notice but that the girl's case seems rather desperate. Because you had a hand in her discovery, I thought you might be better able to uncover how best to help her case," the rector began. He paused, unsure whether to burden the county gentleman with details.

Henry sensed the implied request for permission and felt relieved. He had been unsure whether his wanting to assist the rector would make him more suspect in the neighbor's eyes.

He replied, "I thank you, Reverend LeFebre, for your pains in looking after the young woman in question. I have no doubt that her case is quite desperate from what you wrote and from what I have observed. As to my part in her discovery—" here he hesitated. "I did nothing other than find her when she appeared on the grounds of my estate, the method by which, the police and every member of my household have been unable to discover. In truth, I have been preoccupied with this matter in the past months while the—while Agnes has been in your care, but I have found little further information to resolve her present situation."

A short intake of breath, and then, "But it seems the police have accomplished something by way of intrusive interrogation without consulting you. Perhaps you could tell me more of what you observed?"

"Surely, sir. I was in my study in the back of

the house working on some accounts of the parish rents when I heard screams. They sounded like someone terrified—maybe even someone who'd seen a ghost. Thus alarmed, I went to find the source. I came into the parlor to find Agnes sitting —well, not exactly sitting—she was cowering against the chair, you know, it was terrible—like she was trying to get away from someone striking her."

Here, the Reverend Lefebre paused and gazed at the embroidery chair, and said, "You know, I had always thought she must be a lady that had had a terrible accident befall her, and that her people would eventually find her, but now… now I think maybe she had some evil design acted upon her. Whether she came from quality or a poor crofter family is now, I think, irrelevant. As a Christian, she deserves our pity and the saving grace we can afford her by God's will." He finished and subsided, shaking his head in sadness. Henry judged that the minister did not view the saving grace as being able to restore Agnes to much of the finer points of life.

"What happened with the police after they perceived you were witness to the interview? And what exactly did she—Agnes— reveal in her raving?" Henry asked.

"Well, sir, she was reacting to the questions in a violent manner. Questions about where she was from, I believe. I was not there for any earlier questions, and the police would not tell me anything of what had transpired, except that they were simply asking questions to further the investigation, and thought the hypnotism would get past the amnesia problem. Sergeant Ragby himself was standing in front, holding her in the chair as I entered. I seriously doubt—" but Henry interrupted.

"Very well. The police must have their reasons for secrecy, or confidentiality, if you like. Did they tell you who the hypnotist was, at least?"

"The police did not. It was most rude, not to introduce a guest to the owner of the house, I must say, and it encouraged me to think that what they were doing was not completely above board. However, the housekeeper who showed them in heard the introduction, and Agnes confirmed it. It was a Dr. Tunbridge, from Manchester, of all places!" Lefebre added, exasperated.

"Hmm. Well, I can't say I have heard of the man, but I can certainly make enquiries—discreet enquiries, of course. This matter touches me as much as it does you if not more, since I now believe the police may have me in their sights as a suspect. It may be merely because no other solutions have offered themselves, but any information that I can obtain leading to the truth will both help Agnes and relieve me of having to defend myself."

"Well, Mr. MacFarlane, sir, I trust the Lord

will help uncover the truth of the matter, and I only hope there is a future for our young lady, after she puts this behind her. I fear it will not be soon, but we can always hope and pray. Would it help to talk to Agnes, before she goes away? I'm afraid she is too much prey to nerves in a quiet setting such as the rectory where she has no active occupation. She plans to leave in the next several days for Leeds, to seek employment, and I think it may do her good."

Henry again felt a mild alarm at the immediacy of her plans, having thought he had more time for investigation, but replied smoothly.

"Of course—yes, she may be in danger of losing hope. I have had that in mind these past few months, in fact. Let us see if she can tell us anything more."

Chapter 22

As the housekeeper knocked on the door and entered Agnes' small room, Agnes knew what was coming. She had seen the horse and rider approach, seen the man alight, and had spent the past half-hour wondering what the two men were saying to each other, and how specifically it concerned her. Now at least the agony of expectation was over, and she resolved to remain firm in her decision to leave for Leeds Monday week.

She entered the parlor where she had lately had the interview with the police and that Doctor Tunbridge; it gave her a queer start to recall the visit. The rector and Mr. MacFarlane rose to greet her and she went through the formal niceties in control, her voice smooth.

Mr. MacFarlane broached the subject first. "Mr. LeFebre has just been telling me of the interview that you've had recently, Agnes, and your plans to leave for Leeds. I am deeply sorry to have to see you leave our neighborhood in no greater ease of mind than when you first arrived. I was hoping there might be some way I could assist you in your immediate plans, at least."

"Thank you for your concern, Mr. MacFarlane. I know it means much for you to break up your day to come here in the middle of the business week. I have heard a fair bit from Mrs. Lefebre about how busy you and your brother are, as great titans of industry. You mustn't concern yourself with my problems, since they are likely to be irremovable and their source no doubt undiscoverable. I plan simply to start over, since I have seen little progress in recovering my memory, the police have offered me no more helpful information, and I simply cannot wait any longer. Such is not my temperament. That much I do know," she finished with a ghost of a smile.

"But what will you do? Who will look after you? How will you find work when you've no money? I cannot conceive—"

Agnes cut him off. "No, you cannot conceive of how any of this is to be done, because it can only be done when it must be. Since I must move on, I will. It is something that has been very hard to come to, but I have decided. I would prefer to start again. The police have kindly scouted a lodging place and while they are—" here her voice quivered, "pursuing the case, I shall at least be doing something useful with myself."

The rector opened his mouth to speak, but Henry raised a hand to still him for a moment. He gazed at Agnes, whose spine was ramrod straight, whose hands were clasped together in her lap, whose eyes seemed to glow overbright with purpose. Henry saw she was already out of his reach and had erected a defensive wall against any objections to her decision. He was saddened that there was nothing he could do, with his brother still out of contact, and his hands tied by the police's suspicion. And yet.

"Miss Agnes, there are things about this interview which you do not know. That doctor was not a real doctor but a hypnotist, and you were put — I am sorry, my dear, but I thought you would— oh, my dear..." She had started violently and lost all her hard-won composure, her eyes switching from searing Henry's soul to darting down to the floor. This is what Henry had wanted to prevent.

She raised her eyes to Mr. Lefebre, shivering with the sobs which trickled slowly out as she spoke.

"I—I'm sorry, sir, but I don't know what he's talking about. I don't feel—I don't think I'd like to hear about any hypno—tism," she ground out. "With so little notice and in such company," she tried to say demurely, but ended by sounding disparaging. No matter. Henry knew what she meant. Unfortunately she was the last to know, not he.

"Miss Agnes," he said softly, "Mr. LeFebre has already told me what transpired in his desire for good counsel. If you would—"

But it was no use. She had shut her eyes, covered her face with her hands, and turned her head to the window, fearing a truth she could not formulate. Henry knew he should withdraw for politeness' sake, but could not bring himself to leave her with no relief, or turn his eyes from her quiet, suffering face. He still felt responsible for her, even though she no longer wanted to confide in him.

Chapter 23

Four days later, Agnes was holding a carpet-bag full of secondhand clothes and personal effects, standing on the small train platform for the village of Gilberdyke, the closest stop to the Lefebres' church. Her train was pulling in slowly, steam puffing all around. She wanted to make sure that she found the right car for her direction, so she was closely scrutinizing the names printed on the sides of each as they came into view.

She was herself being scrutinized, and by not one party but two. One party was in uniform, whistling and swinging a billy club. The other party was in a tatty black greatcoat, ambling back and forth, glancing up often in a way that suggested waiting for someone's arrival.

She found her car—No. 6 for Leeds—and walked to the door that was being thrown open by the operator. He looked down, smiling, to ask, "Direction Leeds, miss?"

"Yes, sir," she replied with the faint return of

a smile, and stepped onto the stool he placed before her.

Once on the train, she stowed her valise, removed her coat and hat, and sat wearily down, though it was only eight o'clock in the morning.

"Aye, it's one of those days, isn't it just, miss?" The operator said sympathetically, holding out a hand for her ticket.

"Yes, it is, just."

The train eased out into the open fields immediately outside the station and settled into its repetitive stride, a hypnotic 'ticka-ticka' of the railroad ties. She let herself be lulled into the rhythm, considering what she had learned in the last week, which she had not allowed herself to consider until she was firmly out of the county.

I was hypnotized, she thought. I knew it. I just couldn't bear to think of it. Now does that mean I can get my memories back? And will I want to?

* * *

Although the police had remained silent, maintaining that there were no new leads and no new information, the Lefebres' maid Annie had related to Agnes what she had heard of the interview before she left. It being such a singular occurrence in the parish, she had stayed to listen at the door, and gone right off to fetch her master when Agnes had started crying out in distress.

This showed Agnes two things: that the police had not taken proper precautions to keep their interview discreet, and that they were actively attempting to keep it secret from her. This was distressing news, since it placed the police again firmly outside the very small circle of people she could trust. Did it follow that Henry MacFarlane was back in that circle?

Agnes' thoughts turned to the note he had written to her after their upsetting interview on Thursday. His words had indicated that he felt some amount of concern and regard for her, completely independent of that responsibility which had sprung from the circumstances of her being found in his home. She wasn't sure in what light she should receive that concern and regard, so had chosen to return the note with thanks for his courtesies. She did not yet know what to do about her lodgings, which the police had provided, but which she was certain she should exchange for others as soon as possible, for her safety and peace of mind, such as it was.

She closed her eyes, rested her head and returned to the information Annie had related: her name, her birthplace, and her childhood home. It was so frustrating to know that there was information locked up inside herself, which she herself could not access! She had progressed from amazement at this discovery four days ago, to horror, and was now at patient acceptance. She was not yet bitter, even though the knowledge of her hypnotism must lead to other conjectures. She had closed her mind to the consideration of these matters until she was away from that place, those people, and had started on her new self.

She would begin this new life by using the name she had cobbled together for herself: Agnes Broderick.

Chapter 24

Horace had not yet risen, likely exhausted after the speedy trip back from the North, where he had been making enquiries. Henry decided to let him sleep a few more minutes, then rouse him. Since he had spoken with Lefebre, Henry had been quite busy, and there were now more tasks to be delegated to his brother, to maintain the appearance that things had not changed. He looked at his pocket watch again, and strode from the parlor to Horace's private rooms.

Pausing to knock on the bedroom door, Henry heard a mumbled groan, which he took as assent, and entered the room, where he found his brother in a most unusual position: at his writing-desk. He was not, however, suitably dressed or presentable.

Horace knew his brother to be the visitor, and so waved him over without turning away from what he was writing. When Henry drew near, he saw among the scatter of papers on the desk several train timetables, two maps of the rail lines, a small paper with some hasty writing scratched on it, and many more pages of Horace's scrawled writing in evidence, most of them struck through in their entirety.

After a few moments of not being able to deduce from this agglomeration the genius of the work underway, Henry begged an explanation.

"My strategy to obtain information about missing girls without exciting suspicion was to request information for a publicity on the safety of our rail lines, compared to those of other companies. Its relevance was thin and did not entirely capture the pool of names we want, but I could think of nothing else to start. That is how I received a list of unfortunate girls and women who have disappeared while taking a rail journey, are presumed to have been on a rail journey since they have disappeared, or are otherwise connected with a railway in the manner of their disappearance.

"One of the cities caught my eye, since it was there that I attended a display of mesmerism, given by—"

"A what! did you say?" Henry exclaimed.

"Yes, a display of mesmerism, or what is now called hypnotism. When I received your telegram, it immediately recalled to me an event in Berwick, as the demonstration was so queer and sinister. I attended it on a lark with some friends of mine in northern Yorkshire, but we were all rather put off by the practitioner—or doctor, as he styled himself."

"I will not go into what I think of your judgement in attending such a display, but I fear more information will be divulged that I will not like any more than this, so let's have it, Horace," Henry said tersely.

"In my youth! This was more than five years ago, and of course I realize now that many of them are charlatans, but then it seemed merely a bit of magic and trickery. I did not know—I did not know. And I will finish telling my portion so that we can also hear out your portion, with more on hypnotists!

"Now, as I said, Berwick being on that list caught my eye because of your late and sensational telegram. I have been examining the list of names and places I received with an eye to which rail lines could also have passed through Berwick so that when we look at the descriptions or likenesses, we will have narrowed the pool of possible Agneses. She may have been mixed up with one of these charlatans. If she disappeared recently, in this area, it is a likely hypothesis. So far I have six names from the past ten months that qualify—"

"Are any of them named Euphemia?" Henry asked.

"No, but why do you ask that? Do you know her name?" Horace asked.

"Yes! I could not have trusted that to a telegram, though, of course. I have been waiting for you to wake up so I could tell you what I have discovered, but here it seems you have been working with only half our information! Let us see…"

Chapter 25

From his low seat in the dark corner of Sergeant Ragby's office, Barton stared at the ceiling while he listened to his superior talk himself through the case at hand. He was mightily tired of the mumbling and pacing, and had long since exhausted his ability to contribute by questioning the sergeant, but racked his mind for something.

"Now, now, now..." Ragby rambled.

"Sergeant, might it be the case that she is not in league with anyone, and does simply mean to start over with her life at this point?"

"No, no, my boy. You cannot look at the facts and conclude that, now, can you? She has obviously been trapped and trained for a purpose." Barton gave him a blank look.

"Well, of course she has! Think, sir, of whoever has taken the time to train that young mind to speak a certain way,and not reveal its secrets under trance. They will certainly not just let go of that investment. If we are to, ah, make sure she doesn't fall back into their hands, we shall have to deduce what she was trained for. And by whom. Is there a single spiteful influence, aimed at a personal grudge? Or a bigger scheme, which we must expose and stop? No, sir, one doesn't see this sort of consequence without tracking down the cause: 'twould be dereliction of duty!"

Barton saw that his superior officer was puffing himself up like a freight train, and although he was not persuaded to his conclusion, he prodded him further. "All right, sir, so we do track her movements in Leeds, after I visit Glasgow to ask after her family. Suppose she is innocent: she may feel malevolently watched and fall ill. Suppose she is guilty: she will know not to show herself. And if there is some mastermind guiding her against her will, whether for personal grudge or for some larger cause, he will certainly not reveal himself. So—"

"So where does that leave us, eh? That is what I am thinking through. I can't help but wonder if those MacFarlanes are involved. Because of the need for... discretion, in this case, once you are installed in Leeds, reports will need to come only to me. You, ah, understand?" Ragby stopped speaking, quelling his fidgety manner to impress a look of gravity on the younger man.

Barton inclined his head, wishing he did not understand all that the sergeant had left unsaid: that the control of information in such a potentially

Margaret Pinard

inflammatory scandal would put him in a position to blackmail the brothers.

Chapter 26

The bright lights of the city overwhelmed Agnes at first, and so she kept mainly to her rooms at the lodging house. The police had located it and paid for two days' stay, a fact which motivated Agnes to strike out on the third day to ask directions of the lodger-lady. She ventured down to the nearest market, a ten-minute walk, and observed all she saw with an eye of wonder, not self-conscious in the slightest.

She saw large even pavements, shops of all color and quality, and traffic that careened past at a breakneck pace. She traveled down Beckett Street toward the center of town and passed old, falling-apart tenements, avoiding the gazes of those who stood outside, waiting listlessly. She saw another neighborhood take shape, this one middle-class, mannerly, and stolidly of brick. She slowed to watch many servants pass in the street, recognizing and greeting one another on their errands.

Agnes crossed the York Road and then went

underneath the railway track, keeping in mind the right turn that would take her to the market. Except that she didn't take the right turn, because she caught sight of an immense old church and was drawn to its massive silhouette. Her eyes went over the teeming vertical lines, lines of stone, of carved arch, of tall window. Shall I go in? she asked herself, but the dark grey walls neither invited nor guarded against her.

Maybe another time, she thought, and turned back northward where the market stood. From that moment of decision, where she weighed her wants and desires and felt no pressure to decide one way or the other, she started to relax and enjoy the sights and sounds, laughing in delight when she came to the market and was greeted by a juggler dressed in many bright colors and feigning to drop a pin every third catch.

It was Saturday, and the handsome Kirkgate Market was crowded with shoppers going about their daily business as well as those browsing at the many fancy goods stalls. So this is the nearest market where I could go for some cheese and bread, Agnes laughed to herself. Perhaps Mrs. Brumley has a sense of humor after all! And with that she dove into the crowd, heartily pleased to be so immersed in the lives of others and untroubled by her own problems.

The next day, she rose before dawn to attend

to her toilette, since she had an interview for a lady's maid position in a small but respectable household on The Headrow. Agnes hoped that the position would allow her to move to the neat little house on Quebec Street, as it was closer to the big market, the church, and the town center. She arrived at the servants' entrance on time and was ushered in the back door of the house and made to wait in the kitchen.

It was a fairly large room, with only two servants risen at this time of day, both glancing over at her with leashed curiosity. After they had both finished their breakfast while Agnes watched, the woman who had answered her knock came back with instructions for the day.

"My lady has agreed to speak to you about your trial today. I shall take you upstairs, and if she decides to keep you, I'll show you the house so you know where to go to fetch anything. Follow me."

And the test had started.

Chapter 27

Both of the brothers MacFarlane were looking less scrubbed than their usual professional and charming selves. In the sitting room, Horace leaned back on the arm of a divan looking tired, while Henry strode back and forth across the open space, staring ahead intensely.

"Once more, Horace, in the same order, but leave out that last name, since I think she can be eliminated from consideration," Henry sighed.

"Dundee, December 14, matches description of a young woman missing, name Dolly May Madison; Alnmouth, February 7 or 8, matches description of a young woman missing, name unknown; Penrith, February 15, matches description of two young women missing, names Cornelia Brogan and Edith MacRae; Harrogate, March 4, matches description of a young woman missing, name Elizabeth Surley," Horace finished the recitation, no longer needing to look at his notes, as this was his sixth repeat performance.

"Now, those all offer interesting possibilities, but let's reconstruct what we have so far in terms of motive. We agree that someone deposited Agnes here in order to blacken our family name, possibly out of longstanding malice, possibly out of recent cause for injury. Yes?"

"Yes."

"That leaves us still with many possibilities. But enter in the other facts: the method. The method by which this presumably aggrieved party has chosen to enact their revenge is very circuitous, involving some form of kidnapping, and hypnotism that induces amnesia into the bargain! It may also involve cooperation with the police since an investigation would be even worse than country gossip, but we've no proof of that yet. But the fact they are refusing to talk to us rather indicates they suspect us, which is aggravating. Agreed?"

"Agreed."

"Leaving aside the potential for a larger purpose of the hypnosis-amnesia, we should consider that it would take some amount of time to isolate the woman, separating her from help, conquering her mind, etc."

Here, Henry had paused in his circuit of the center rug, and the fingers of his right hand were stabbing against his palm as he refused to voice what else might have been conquered. His flow of logic always got stuck amid those feelings of rage and righteous anger that he had tried so hard to control since he had first heard the story of the hypnosis interview at the rectory. Rage against people who wanted to harm his family and property, and against those who would use a young woman like Agnes for evil. His brother sensed this even with his eyes closed, and to keep the rational part of his brother going, he interjected.

"Agreed. Which is why I had that worm Kincaid go back six months or so for kidnappings on the rail lines north, where she was most likely taken, given the information the police extracted. Are you thinking a different timeline is now more probable?"

"No, hold on, that is another possibility I have set aside, but I have not gotten to the end of the first, easiest flow of events. Possible events." Henry paused. "We don't believe she can have been used for anything before being deposited here, do we? At least in this neighborhood? We would have heard of anything untoward or out of the ordinary, would we not? And once she'd been exposed in such a way, she could hardly do the same again in the same neighborhood."

"You would have heard, surely."

"All right. Then, unless the perpetrators of this crime, who have no love for us, have taken her hither and yon experimenting, it is likely that six months or fewer might be sufficient. Now, on to the less likely possibilities. If there is a larger purpose for this hypnosis training, we may be a mere pawn, the perpetrator a villain of a much larger scene, and this merely a handy experiment for him. What do you think of that possibility, Horace?"

"Bollocks. Somehow those people who are in Father's will are involved—that's what I think."

"Which people? The family who were given rights to the cottage down by the old mill house? Or—"

"Yes, the Dennys. Two years ago, the will made reference to earlier amounts handed over to them, which I can in no way account for, business-wise. I passed you those a week ago; have you had any luck?"

"Er—no, I can't say I was able to check them, I'm sorry. I shall do that tomorrow. I haven't had much time to spare in the past month. This has consumed so much time in investigating covertly, while I've had to attend to all the regular boards and committees' concerns as usual. I've—" and here he emitted a jaw-cracking yawn. "I've had just too much. Too much of this," he finished simply, and plopped down next to Horace on the sofa. "What time is it, anyway?"

Horace checked his pocket watch. "Quarter past two."

"Start again in the morning, shall we? And dream about how to get our next scrap of information."

Chapter 28

"Yes, my lady."

"No, my lady."

The parroted phrases rang in her head as she recounted her responses. Agnes had the odd feeling of déjà vu in remembering her answers to the police many weeks before. She had much higher hopes, though, for the outcome of this interview, than she had now for the other. At the moment, she was seated in the empty outer kitchen room of the house on Quebec Street, the residence of Sir Hereford Worley and his wife Lady Helen.

As Agnes waited for the conclusion of the interview between the housekeeper and the lady of the household, she wondered about the functioning of such a house, its circulation, regulation, hierarchy. There were only four serving staff and not a large household, so things seemed to run smoothly. The housekeeper who had greeted her upon entry had an iron discipline and a face to match, but seemed fair: a Mrs. Kingsley. No mention of a Mr.

Kingsley. And no telling how long it would be before I find out about that, Agnes thought.

At the end of an hour, the cook started to make some noise in the inner kitchen room, which held the giant oven and range, the sinks, and the shelves with foodstuffs and preparatory tools. As the preparation noises for lunch grew steadier, Mrs. Kingsley returned from above-stairs. She came to Agnes, who rose and looked her in the eye.

"You've got your trial, and you can start as soon as you've changed into a uniform. Be good if you could help with lunch as well." She handed her a pile of clothes consisting of a black skirt, a white shirtwaist and a white apron, nodding at her to follow as she turned to exit the room.

"You can use this space for the day," Mrs. Kingsley said, indicating a door on the left of the servants' hallway, "And before you leave, we will let you know whether you are to return to stay. Have you any questions?"

"No, I mean, yes, Mrs. Kingsley. That is, I am not familiar with the house, and have not properly met the other staff. May I be permitted to do so before serving?"

"Yes, of course. I will handle that as soon as you've changed and come back to the outer kitchen."

"Thank you."

She had been honest in answering all the

questions, and private about her earlier life, which she supposed had led Lady Helen and the others to believe that she was just a country bumpkin that did not know 'town' manners and duties. That suited her fine. At last Agnes would have an occupation, and a place.

* * *

Lady Helen was conversing with her husband before lunch in their upstairs rooms, since he had had his appointment in town postponed.

"She has such nice references from the country minister that I thought it would do no harm to give her a try, especially as your associate wants her to find a good place," Lady Helen said.

"He's not an associate, dear, more like an acquaintance... but one to whom I owe a small favor, to be frank. I appreciate your goodwill in engaging her. Even if it doesn't work out well, I shall still be out from under the obligation of the favor. But if it does, you shall have a new maid, and that will be that," said Sir Worley.

"Yes, well, seeing that there is no 'down side,' as you like to say, I will give myself to hope that there is a substantial 'up side.' She is quite pleasant and obliging. I think she will be fine after some training, which I will suffer through," she said, teasingly.

Sir Hereford arrested his worrisome thoughts and gazed in appreciation at his wife, all her matronly curves, her thirty-three years, her rich golden hair, her playful wit. He had to remind himself again how blessed he was to have found her. And her dowry.

"I thank you for that, my dear. I hope she becomes accustomed quickly, for your sake, then. And then we may be able to talk again about that addition to the house," he said, with a not well-hidden eagerness.

"Oh no, you don't!" Lady Helen said playfully, "that would be such a racket, and I told you, I'd need to be away for the duration. There is no way I could accustom myself to that amount of noise and discomfort, and no reason to. We have no need of a verandah around the back. Let those Filberts deal with theirs, and that, as you say, will be that," she ended on a clever note, throwing his words back at him.

Sir Hereford harrumphed his amusement.

At lunch, Agnes flitted in and out of the dining room, following Mrs. Kingsley's instructions to the letter, humble and happy to see that it would not be a bad situation here at all. Lady Helen was pleased by her quick eye and hand, and Sir Hereford Worley seemed oblivious, remarking on the pleasant taste of the smoked ham and the next morning's appointment with his 'acquaintance.'

Mrs. Kingsley was pleased, but no one

would have known.

* * *

As Agnes walked back to her lodgings that evening before the dinner hour to collect her things, she walked with an air of dreaming. She thought of what she had learned that day, filing it in the drawers of her mind for quick reference. She thought of what she had learned the day before, proud of becoming familiar with the main streets in her neighborhood. She found she wasn't frightened by the noise, the activity, or the potential dangers that came along with city living. She observed this and pondered it in a quiet state.

Very soon she was passing by the old grey church again, and gazed at its windows, now gleaming with the setting rays of the sun. She decided to circle the outside, as it was now closed, its ponderous doors shut and padlocked until the next morning's services.

There was the paved walkway, the green lawns, the view of the cemetery, and then her breath caught—Why, there's the river! Agnes quickly changed her plan and dashed between the parish buildings to get a wider view of the River Aire, which she'd glimpsed through the trees and bricks. The river made hardly any noise, flowing swiftly underneath the surface. There was a large bridge to her left, but Agnes left that for another time, instead enjoying the sight of the dark, smooth water.

She passed several quiet minutes standing there on the sloping lawn looking toward the river. It settled her heart somehow.

Is it like the Clyde? she wondered, remembering from that awful interview that she'd been raised in Glasgow's Clyde Valley. A slow heat burned behind her eyes as she thought of it, and caused a few tears to trickle down. She closed her eyes and took a steadying breath. With it, she took in the grassy smells of the river, the slight cool breeze on her cheek. She heard a sharp cry off to her left and opened her eyes, dousing instantly the hint of a memory that had been creeping back: being beside a river like this, on a warmer day. When? Where? Why did I leave? she asked herself angrily. Why did I ever leave, if only to end up here?

She tried to close her eyes and coax the memory back, but it had fled. She sighed, wiped her cheeks, and turned from the water to return to the lodging house.

As she clung to the minute memory and felt the movement of the city behind her, she did not notice when two uniformed policemen turned as she did, following her, for several blocks.

Chapter 29

Henry perused the papers Horace had given him a fortnight before; they gave him the feeling that his mind was being run through a maze. One document contained the signature of his father; he could tell it had been written after his father was taken ill as it shook and faded at the end. In it, his father, Charles Windsom MacFarlane, had arranged for the widow of a game warden of the property to inherit the cottage where the warden and his family had lived. This had caught his attention since some of the receipts had been intermingled.

In another of the documents, Henry saw his own signature, acquiescing to the execution of the will and its contents after his father's death.

These two were nothing in and of themselves but notary files, and rendered nothing useful in connecting what had happened then with what had happened more recently, namely, a young woman being hypnotized and dropped at his door. His bathroom door, no less.

What Horace had theorized about the receipts' origin was complex but not unimaginable: that there had been some indiscretion on their father's part, and that the warden's wife knew, and that she had extracted a promise of the cottage property for her family in exchange for silence. Lord MacFarlane had been known to be outgoing and to enjoy the company of women, but in the two years since the patriarch's death neither of his sons had heard any whispers of actual deeds.

Other than those two papers, Horace had included the following: a receipt at Locanza's Fabric & Fittings from September 1876, two years before their father's death, for £18; a receipt for a subscription to the Goole Public Library for the 1876 year; the purchase of two interest-bearing shares in the East India Company, a most successful colonial enterprise, dated even earlier: August 17, 1872.

It had been Henry's task to reply to all the open accounts upon their father's death, but he had not seen, or at least not remembered, these. He made a mental note to check his own record of those months, but first, something was niggling at him, something larger than Horace's insinuation that these receipts related to the alleged indiscretion. No, it was a memory trying to make its way to his attention, rising through the muck of more recent and more powerful memories...

When it came, Henry stared open-mouthed at the stack of papers, realizing he would have to go through a good many more.

* * *

The memory that had come to him was a chance comment made one breezy day when he and his father had been together in the fields to see how the new tilling technique was coming along. They were watching the combine being pulled along by the drays, seeing in its wake not only the furrowed rows but also a light-colored powder being spread in between: a lime byproduct coming out of the Welsh mines that was supposed to be good for the soil.

"Makes you wish they had the same stuff for seeds growing up into young men, just," his father had expressed with some chagrin.

Henry had turned to his father, wondering if he should be offended on Horace's behalf, but saw that his father's eyes were staring into the long distance, thinking of something far away. He waited.

"Something about starting over on a new child—" but he seemed to recollect himself. "Ah, Henry, I'm glad to be your father, and I'll be happy to see you well married and with a healthy brood. That's all I meant to say. You'll do well."

Henry knew, musing in the present, that if his father had had more than 'an indiscretion,' and had actually fathered a child, he would feel honor-bound to provide for it. What Horace had compiled might be evidence of an affair. That, combined with his fleeting memory, might be indication of an illegitimate child, but it could just as well be nothing.

He fell to sorting through the five-year-old stacks of records in the study, studying the receipts that could now be evidence of a scandal, wondering about the sort of man his father had been, and the sort of father.

Agnes drifted to the background.

Chapter 30

That day, a young policeman in Leeds was contemplating the change of seasons, with late spring succumbing to the insistent heat of summer. This meant he would have to start changing his wool uniform more often, which annoyed him. This would be his first summer on the Force, and he wanted it to be all swish authority and promotions but he was finding it wasn't that way at all. Damned itchy, awfully boring for long stretches, and involving a lot of boot-licking, as far as Private Wendell was concerned.

But he had happened on a sideline of work that might help him to a promotion earlier than anticipated: a sergeant from a neighboring county had asked him to keep an eye on a suspect, in return for a good word with his supervisor, come September. He'd had a week of it, ending his rounds where she worked and following her on the afternoon errands she had around town. It was none too bothersome, and the girl had a nice figure to keep an eye on, come to that. Just now, he was taking a break at a bar around the corner from her lodgings.

Wendell wondered what she was suspected of doing, but not for long. His mind drifted to the other private he had enlisted to watch her, Private Nichols, who did not have a morning shift. He wouldn't get a good word, but he might— might— get an introduction to Wendell's sister. He grinned at his cleverness in cheating Nichols, then turned to ask for another beer from the barman.

* * *

The shift to warmer weather was not borne the same way by everyone in the bustling city of Leeds, however. Lady Helen was preparing to re-move to her family's country house, known as Clatteringshaws, where the Worleys had summered since their marriage. They shared it with its perma-nent residents, Lady Helen's two unmarried sisters.

Agnes learned a great many details during this preparation, including the garments that would be needed for the summer in the country, which were, of course, different from a summer in the city, how to care for them, which jewelry to take, where to lock the remainders, etc.

Agnes was at least certain of her ability to address any sewing-related issues while at the country house, but the constant changing of clothes and rearranging of hair was something to which she was not habituated, and always seemed to pass in a flurry. She was making progress in anticipating Lady Helen's needs, however, which helped. And even though she had just come from the country herself, she was excited to see her employers' country home, which certainly sounded luxurious from their description of it, kept in style as it was by the maiden aunts—Dowager Baronesses, no less.

They would be traveling by coach to High Bentham, the village in northwestern England closest to the estate. It was possible to journey there by train on the North Western Railway in relative comfort, but Agnes was just as glad not to be stuffed into a metal coach tram. The personal servants of the Worleys would need to pack carefully, put everything to order behind them, and accompany the carriage, with Agnes on the box seat, and Stanley the valet seated behind. It would be a journey of about seventy miles, over three leisurely days, with a stop in the Yorkshire Dales. Lady Helen would in fact be making the journey alone because of some meetings that her husband had in Birmingham, so she wanted to stop and enjoy the countryside on the way.

Agnes was pleased with her own aptitude; she liked working for Lady Helen, and Mrs. Kingsley had even paid her the compliment that she was a 'quick learner.' Stanley had asked her a few friendly questions about home, a practice which, after not having them answered, he quickly discontinued, but he remained civil enough.

Sir Hereford did not have much occasion to speak to her, but in the fortnight since she had started, he had made a point of watching her at certain times. It unnerved her a bit, but she chalked it up to feeling behind or negligent in her duties, and always followed it by asking Mrs. Kingsley if there was anything she could do.

All in all, things seemed to be working out for the new Agnes Broderick.

* * *

Sergeant Ragby's assistant Barton peered into the pub on the warm June afternoon. He himself had not been bribed into doing this extra bit of side work. He now knew all the details in the Yorkshire part of this tale, as well as a few corroborating facts from the Glasgow end. He was acting as a detective for Sergeant Ragby on this errand. He'd been sent to find the bobby assigned to watch over their subject. Although Ragby had told him that she was a suspect in a case, Barton thought privately it was more likely she was being used as bait.

He spotted Wendell from Ragby's description: tall, sparing frame, thin, brown hair, and a face like a spoiled child. Yep, this was him, all right.

Barton did his best to blend in with the city

crowd, dressed as he was a bit differently and not knowing the regulars. He casually made his way to the bar and to the side of Mr. Wendell.

"Hullo there, man. You Wendell?" he said quickly, trying to sound like he was chuffing a pal.

"Yes, sir. And you must be—" but Barton interrupted, "Cousin of Jerry's, tha's right." And he proceeded to gab and drink and siphon information about the lad's latest case.

Chapter 31

The country around High Bentham was even more beautiful than that Agnes had recently left behind her at the Lefebres', and so she enjoyed the scenery and the warm weather outdoors when she could, a few minutes at a time during the day. She was settling in well with her family, and thought she might enjoy the steady job. Now for the long stretch, she thought.

As the country stay progressed through its eight weeks, Agnes felt those surges of memory and emotion she used to have sink into the distance. She assumed more duties, was less supervised at more sophisticated tasks, and developed a polite, friendly discourse with the valet.

With Her Ladyship, Agnes was encouraged in terms of her personal capability and taste, but the lady-to-maid relationship was not one that encouraged her to smile either. Agnes wondered if this was what she had been born into, whether this subservience was her natural station, and how much one's character depended on the circumstance in which one finds oneself. She would find herself daydreaming from time to time about being the lady of the house, then chide herself for engaging in thoughts that could only lead to unhappiness. It was a steady position, to be sure.

Not once had she noticed the weekly visitors to the house who never entered. A couple of local Cumbrian policemen were put on the job as soon as Wendell and Nichols were robbed of their convenient quarry in Leeds. A rotation of a two local policemen at the road through which all carriages had to pass to approach the park maintained this watch without alerting the house's occupants.

The eight weeks seemed to pass slowly for these watchers, except for one who arrived late, halfway through the stay. This one, a detective from down Leeds way, was more familiar with the details of the case and had begun to suspect something darker, the country whispers spurring his imagination.

Chapter 32

On one of her free half-hours, Agnes had stolen out early one morning to the pond. It was very large and some distance from the house, about fifteen minutes' walk. The sun was just barely up, but she knew the household to be generally asleep, as the dinner party the night before would slow everyone's desires to be industrious today.

The pond sat behind a small hill, tilted away from the view of the house. It was surrounded by reeds and water-plants, and it was into these that she crept now, carefully removing her shoes and stockings and dangling her feet into the cool water. She leaned back onto the bank, conscious of keeping her shift and coat clean.

Agnes looked up to see the clouds shaded from grey to pink to white, marveling at their slow rolling pace and ever-changing colors. A sigh escaped her, and as she heard it, it became a hiccup. She felt giddy with joy for this moment, when she could appreciate where she was, without worrying about who she was, or was not.

She thought about her name and birth-city again, as she had many times in the past weeks. She thought of her mother. Might I not enquire after an Alice Broderick at the Glasgow police station by post? Or after I have some savings, have someone check into the family situation before I venture to visit? I do so wish to know if I still have family left there.

A breeze rustled through the reeds and spun the clouds still further. Yes, that is what I shall do. Write to the city police. If they have no answer in a month, I'll find someone to enquire for me, then I'll make a visit. With that point settled, she closed her eyes, sighing again, content for the moment.

Later that day, Agnes learned that Clattering-shaws would be hosting a ball the seventh week of the Worleys' visit, to which a half-dozen good families in the neighborhood were to be invited. The servants of Clatteringshaws were in quite a state of agitation, cleaning and clearing, decorating and preparing. As a middle-aged, established couple, the Worleys felt it was their responsibility to provide the opportunity for yet more prosperous matches to be made, just as theirs had been. The cook at the Park was constantly being summoned for menu changes, and the Dowager Baronesses were consulted on the preferences and habits of the neighboring families. The surfaces were dusted, the woodwork and silver polished, and the rugs beaten within an inch of their lives.

The Dowager Baronesses, Eliza and Paulina, having become accustomed to this sort of barrage over the past two summers, did their best to stay in good temper and not step on the toes of their sister Helen, to whose goodwill they owed their permanent residence. Helen, at thirty-three years of age, was the most ebullient, and Eliza and Paulina, at thirty-four and thirty-seven, regarded her when they were together as one would a golden calf: one who had found a husband who could save the family estate through canny investments. They were ever tender toward Helen and always deferential to their brother-in-law, about whom they still knew only a little. He appeared to them as the gallant partner to their savior, a large gentleman who had the winds of chance at his beck and call.

He did seem lucky, they had murmured to each other many a time, upon hearing through Helen's letters that he had turned a profit on this or that business deal, usually in the jute or coal or wool trades. They chalked it up to his good head for business, and indeed, it was quite a large head, with a full share of shaggy brown hair. He always looked a bit windblown, even when he hadn't been outside. He charmed Pauline most exquisitely when he complimented her pianoforte skills, singing softly along with the sisters. Yes, the summer visits were an occasion to look forward to, and the balls the past two summers had been a source of entertainment for all.

Besides the odd early morning walk, there was usually a lull in Agnes' duties each afternoon, as Lady Helen typically rested in her salon. Agnes sometimes had an hour or more in which to walk outside and enjoy the forest paths and the warm evening air, and she felt herself soaking it in, feeling stronger and healthier as the weeks passed.

On one of these walks, she came to a new spot, a clearing that rose a little from the forest floor. It was not enough to see above the tree-tops, but enough to make the ground dry and firm. She picked her way to the top of the little hill and sat on her coat, wrapping her arms around her knees and gazing eastward, where the dusk had yet to appear. She rested her head on her arms and felt lulled to sleep by the low murmur of water and sweet slow trill of the birds. She thought of home, where her thoughts easily flew these days.

She played the piano by copying someone else's hands. She did excellent needlework, having been taught by her mother, Alice. She felt the strong pull to return and discover more, but was afraid of what else she might find in her past, and so resolved to wait on the letter to the Glasgow police until the family's return to Leeds.

Chapter 33

Horace stared at his brother, shocked and open-mouthed. The wheels started turning again soon, though, and he glanced down, bringing his hand to his chin and setting his elbow on the writing table.

"But then—" Horace started, then stopped.

"It may just be crazy conjecture, Horace, and I am offering it only as a possibility—"

"Yes, but the possibility—after all that he castigated me for!—the possibility that he had a child, a secret family, with—well. I did think of a dalliance, but bringing up the child like his own, visits? This is quite—it's sickening. I thought of the family blackmailing him for an affair, but not this, and with—Let's hear how you discovered it, dismiss it, then move on to the hypnotist angle, please."

Henry looked at his brother, taken aback momentarily. This wasn't the reaction he had expected. Brief surprise, yes, but not such… disgust.

"The beneficiary of the East India Company shares was the widow in the hunting cottage. Her name is Alice Denny. Mrs. Denny was also the customer on the fabric account for which you showed me the receipts. I have asked Arthur what is generally known about this tenant, and he did not have much to say. 'Very quiet, even in the village church, takes close care of her child, a young boy, doesn't take him to the village often, slight frame.' If that is all Arthur knows, that is all anybody knows at the house, of that I'm fairly certain."

"So we have a dearth of information on her habits, but we have evidence of Father's giving to her generously in his will," Henry continued. "I have also remembered something Father said that may indicate that he had an illegitimate child after Mother died. It's all very circumstantial, I agree, which is why we're talking about it first, before investigating any further." Henry paused, eyeing Horace's expression, which was still stony and agitated.

Another thought came to Henry. "And there is the slight connection of the name Alice."

Horace's expression changed, his confusion at the connection evident. "Who—"

"The girl," Henry replied. "Our amnesiac thought for a time it was her name, because she had some sort of strong attachment to it."

"But what could that attachment be?"

"She thought Alice was her mother's name."

"But they're but a few years apart—she couldn't be her mother!"

"And how are you so sure of that, Horace?" Henry eyed his brother sharply, now guessing why he had seemed so inappropriately enraged by the idea of his father taking the cottage girl for a mistress: Horace had. "Never mind it. I can guess. I should have known not to assume there was anything in skirts for miles around with which you wouldn't be familiar."

"Henry, please, don't play so high and mighty with me. We both know why you're really doing this, this search."

After a moment, and without looking up from the papers on the desk, Henry said, "Very well. Let's have a sleep and come back together once we're rested, shall we? Good night." Henry turned from his brother, rose stiffly, and left the room.

* * *

Alone in his bedchamber, Arthur done with his duties, Henry paced back and forth in his dressing gown, worried about what might be happening and anxious about what to do. If Horace was correct about the cottage-woman's age, then the 'Alice' lead was a dead end, unless Agnes was remembering incorrectly, or perhaps even the cottage-woman was involved in some plot against them? She would have had plenty of opportunity to blackmail the family, having been with both father and son. Or perhaps just the son... No, he chided himself, now you're not making any sense whatsoever.

His mind spun in circles around the same sources of weakness, the same points of improper behavior, where Henry had not been involved, but where he would now have to defend the family's name so that rumors of impropriety did not enter the wrong ears and sour some business deal just as it was to be cemented.

Currently a gentleman's agreement for Mac-Farlane Lines was being made into a standing contract, ready for signing, to start shipping jute out of Dundee in the next month, which required the investors in the rail board to vote for it. If they had him thrown off the board, he'd be nothing but a worker in a company of his father's own making, a fate he didn't want to contemplate. And what would get him thrown off the board? Being cited as a criminal witness—or even a suspect!—God help him. Neither he nor Horace had been able to do much to influence the police in this investigation.

The police of the area seemed content to leave the matter where it was, with Agnes in the lurch and any further investigating up to the Mac-Farlanes.

The leads they had tried, tracing Agnes from

any of a number of places from which she might have been kidnapped, were not going well, with none of the cases or descriptions answering to her fair, rosy skin and long curling red hair, her large, dark eyes and her thin, worried mouth...

This night her image had come back to haunt him, but it also gave him courage to continue the search. He privately admitted that Horace's accusations of his having feelings for Agnes might have been true that first day. He had felt protective of her.

He didn't want to make her his wife, though, or even a mistress. He still felt that protective shadow; he yearned to clear away that nervous, scared expression from her face. To see her glow with good health and high spirits.

First on the list was to send away her entreating image, then to figure out how to learn of any progress the police might have made, and meanwhile to continue searching through the list of missing girls' names. Perhaps pay a policeman in Leeds to keep tabs on her. As he slipped into sleep, Henry had a sinking feeling there was more blackness to discover in this affair.

Chapter 34

Constable Norris, back on his normal farmer-and-villager rounds, was nevertheless still thinking about the scintillating case that had for the first time in a long time required him to use the detective skills he remembered from his academy days. He was still miffed that the sergeant hadn't let him explain how he had secured a medical expert himself—and it wasn't because he followed the blinking 'science,' either!

He wondered what the doctor had been able to find out, if anything, and wished still to be 'in the know' on the case. He felt somewhat downcast at the younger and more citified Barton being assigned to the case, and when it included travel, too! Norris had no missus or family to mind and would have liked to be able to see the city again. Why, it had been ages since he'd gone to Leeds, for a family funeral, it was.

He wondered if he could not have done better with that hypnotist mumbo-jumbo chap, though.

After that dismal interview with Sergeant Ragby, Norris had written to thank Doctor Tunbridge and tell him further assistance would not be needed due to a slight change in the case. The fellow had reacted quite strangely, almost rudely, calling into question Norris' wits, the police force's competence, and threatening to complain at having been ill-used. Really, it was quite a carrying-on for someone he had only once contacted and met in person briefly as a potential expert witness in a case. Then Norris had learned that he had already done an interview with their subject Agnes, but Ragby had not told him. That did not sit well with Norris, and Ragby's repeated rebuffs about the case really had gotten to him.

He turned down the lane, brow still furrowed in thought, when he ran into Fred Filchy, an old friend from school and stablehand at Atwell for the MacFarlanes.

"Well, fancy meeting you here, mate, how is't with you?" asked Fred.

"Oh, fine, fine, jus' thinking a bit on a case, you know. How are you getting along, Fred? Been a long while, I gather—your little one's fair grown by now, I imagine?"

"Oh aye, Sally's an imperious girl of three now, and my Sarah's got another one on the way, God grant it be a boy."

"Fine, that's fine. How are things up at the

big house? New stock to speak of?" asked Norris.

"Oh, you know, they've no need for the hunters so much any more, but we've some fine carriage horses last year up on the farm. Very good, they are. Put on a nice show now and again. We should go have a pint and a sit-down—have ye time? They're not having you on any secret murder cases now, are they?" Fred said, joking.

"Ach, no, no such thing in our part of the world, you know that. Jus' some strange things, is all. Some strange things to think about."

"Well, let's stop and have a drink and think then. Good pastime for two men in their prime, eh?"

They settled down in the village pub with their two pints. Norris knew he couldn't mention any of the specifics of the case, but he was just dying to tell someone what he'd been looking into and how daft it all was. So he told Fred he was working on a case that they had over at the University in Grantham, learning about people hoodwinked by hypnotism, and having to talk to this man Tunbridge, who'd been pestering him about the science of mesmerism.

"I mean, honestly," Norris started. "It's one thing if I call him to ask questions in the pursuit of justice. It's another thing if he calls me back, telling me to ask him more questions—strange, no? And asking me questions about the case! That's not on, is it? Everyone knows about the confidentiality of investigations, and I was just doing my part."

"Course you were, Archie. We know you're honest, and you had to turn the man away. We'll always have the busybody sort, it seems… although 'round here it's less likely to be a doctor of letters and more to be the aldermen's wives," he said, calming his friend's agitation and trying to put him in a good humor again. "Don't worry a bit more about it. I'm sure your sergeant is taking care of it all, running hither and yon for justice. Yes, we each do our part. Mine is to keep those horses healthy and shiny as a new penny; yours is to investigate whose chickens got into whose parlor and which laws we're breaking by breathing—oh come, Archie, I'm just teasin' ye. You know it's half-true anyway, friend," he said with a sly grin.

"Well, I will leave that unanswered, but I do appreciate the catching up, Fred. Ought to be back on my way now. Give my love to the missus," Norris returned, rising and re-entering the misty street a bit more light-hearted.

* * *

In the way of country conversations, Fred had mentioned this sensational bit of news about Archibald Norris being involved with a bloomin' hypnotist to Nell the parlor maid, and she had gossiped it to Harriet the housemaid, and she had repeated it to the cook while Arthur the valet had been listening. He took the news to Mr. MacFarlane at the first opportunity the next morning.

"You're saying that Constable Norris said that a hypnotist had been contacting him about the case involving the girl here?"

Arthur followed his master's pacings back and forth in the room. "Yes, sir."

"So, not only has the sergeant had a hypnotist in to interview Agnes, but the police constable has also been interviewing the hypnotist? This is very perplexing. What can they be thinking? Of course I need not be privy to all the investigation's details, but the bits I am hearing certainly tend to drain away any confidence I had that they were doing their duty!"

Henry made an effort to slow his breathing. "I'm sorry, Arthur, I'm getting heated. I appreciate your canny ears, and especially your tact in passing this piece of news to me. Horace and I haven't gotten very far doing our own investigating, so this news of where the police are heading is making me sore."

He sighed. "Well, we shall see what this brings us. I am going to think a bit more on it and perhaps contact the constable or the sergeant. I'll be in the library most of the day then and would like not to be disturbed until tea."

"Yes, sir."

* * *

It had been almost a week since Horace and Henry's tense conversation wherein Henry had discovered that Horace's   weakness strayed far closer to home than was comfortable. Horace had either stayed in his chamber or gone out riding to the far reaches of the parklands to avoid his brother, but he had come 'round enough to consider the possibility that the woman he had thought of as his mistress might also have been his father's.

It was a terrible thought, and he hoped at least that much time had separated the encounters. But even allowing for that possibility, it didn't solve the mystery of the age proximity of Agnes and his Alice. If Alice could not be Agnes' mother, was it just two completely separate opportunities for outsiders to blackmail the MacFarlane family? That was a terrifying thought.

Horace had puzzled over this enough to want an answer, but when he had gone as far as the piece of land on which the old gamekeeper's cottage stood, he'd been informed by a passing farmer that the inhabitants, Alice and her son, were off visiting relatives for a midsummer festival.

Unable to resolve that uncertainty for the moment, Horace had decided to return to the house and confront his brother, if necessary. As he rode back to the great house, a post rider was just leaving the front courtyard. His curiosity piqued, he handed the horse off to a groom and immediately queried the butler whether there was new mail.

"Yes, Master Horace, the post has just come from London with some mail that was left at your club for you."

Receiving it from Moyers' hand, Horace remarked, "I wouldn't wonder that people might have thought I would be back in town before now, but... well, circumstances have been intervening," Horace said.

"Yes, sir. There are also some letters that came from the county mail, mostly for your brother."

"All right, thank you, Moyers. I'll be in the east study."

Chapter 35

Clatteringshaws was the height of sophistication for the night of the ball, as far as the residents in the local vicinity were concerned. There were lights at each of its front-facing windows, and flowers decorating a trellis on both sides of its front entrance. Six different families of standing had been invited, for a total of nine unmarried women and seven unmarried men, which promised great entertainment for Lady Helen and mild annoyance for Sir Hereford. He was always more concerned about the potential for drama than he was interested in the younger set's lives, but Lady Helen was much enjoying her role as encourager of romances.

She had chosen her newest gown and saved it to wear first at this ball, for it complemented her complexion and hair very nicely. Agnes had pressed the blue silk with a light hand, careful of the pulls that kept the bustle in the back stable and smooth. She was now working with Lady Helen's hair, smoothing down the small pieces that had come loose from the low comb holding back her long, fine hair.

Lady Helen was speculating on the dancing partners to Agnes, "And that Mr. Scott had better stand up for a dance or two with Miss Elliot after what her parents did for his sister in town. I hope Miss Elliot will have more than one admirer, though, being so good-hearted as she is. Now, Mr. Joseph Bellingham might be just the type..." she pattered.

Agnes was excited to see all the preparations, decorations, and menus, but she would be most relieved after Lady Helen was on the floor and out of her hands. She looked very fine, but still wanted some fussing over, which Agnes wasn't sure how to do without ruining her own work.

At last her lady was done with her breathless anticipating, and she joined Sir Hereford to welcome guests that were just arriving. Agnes crept to a position in a dark hallway above the open ballroom where she could survey the whole scene.

There was the receiving line. There was the band, all set up with its shiny brass and polished wood instruments. Here was the punch table already attended by a couple of young men, fetching drinks, certain of their partners. Along the opposite wall were the large paintings that Sir Hereford had collected on recent travels, displayed for the first time before this company. Agnes expected everyone would be obliged to circulate past them and pass some comment to the hosts. It felt so familiar.

She sighed and shook off the feeling, as she had the rare others in the past two months of this summer visit. Better just to enjoy the spectacle and not endlessly tempt her mind into that dark, yawning cavern whence no thought ever returned.

Chapter 36

Horace was enjoying the letters from friends in London and had almost forgot his decision to face the hard dealings with Henry, when his brother entered from the east hall.

"Are we back to reasonable men again?" Henry said, eyeing his brother.

"Yes, Henry. Let's proceed. I've gone through my mail. No new information. You might want to check yours."

Henry picked up the small parcel of letters, flipping through them, relegating them to a few piles, able to guess the contents of each. One bore no return direction, though, so he opened it on the spot.

As Henry's eyes scanned the single page, his brother saw his breath become short, his color pale, and his eyebrows knit together fiercely.

"Henry! What on earth is it! Sit down before you burst into pieces!" he exclaimed, pushing a chair behind Henry's knees.

Follow classic path of mercenary tennis

Henry sank into it slowly, still gripping the page, rereading. "Of all—and the police—this goddamned—"

"Easy, Henry, calm down. Let's get you a glass of something." He rose to retrieve the decanter of port in the corner cupboard, filled a small glass, and returned to Henry's chair.

"Now, what is such a matter as to make you turn blue so quickly? Has it something to do with the company?"

Henry read the short missive, making an effort to unclench his jaw.

This is the prologue. If you don't want the power of our knowledge to be unleashed, do the following: sell all of your firm's holdings in rail lines north of London to Mr. Wakefield of Berwick. If you fail to do so by the First of September, we will alert the papers.

A silence followed Henry's bitten-out words.

Horace gazed at Henry, calculating. Henry no longer knew what he gazed at, his eyes blurry with tears of rage and frustration.

"Then it is come. Do you have any—" Horace started, and was cut of by his brother.

"No. But I will find out. Before September. And without the police."

* * *

Sergeant Ragby had only said to supervise the girl's bobbies in Leeds, but when the family left for the country, Detective Barton chose to follow them. By the time he arrived, the Worleys had only a few weeks left at their country estate before returning to town. A sound enough plan for a holiday, as long as you can stomach your in-laws' family, Barton thought. Barton was not so encumbered, and had not felt the need to marry just yet.

However, his status was not serving him well in his career. He knew people thought him shifty when they realized he didn't have a hen pecking at him in the evenings. He was hoping that cracking this important case would land him somewhere closer to town, where he could put more of his detective skills to use, and have a chance at a real career.

In the meantime, he was following this lead to see what developed. He'd made some interesting discoveries on his trip to Glasgow.

Her family had been easy enough to locate. According to them, the girl (he did not call her Agnes) had vanished two years ago, on her way home from staying with relatives in Lanarkshire.

He'd told the parents only that the police might have found a clue to her whereabouts, choosing not to let on that she'd been found, since in any event Agnes herself hadn't decided to return to them. Maybe she didn't want to be found now.

Barton really didn't know what to think of that.

The poor parents were reluctant to speak of her habits and her character to him, believing as they did that she was dead. The mother's name was, indeed, Alice.

There were younger siblings as well, and Barton talked to the next oldest sister Judith, for the space of a few moments while waiting for her mother to fetch the tea-things.

Judith appeared more hopeful than the rest at his appearance, and volunteered a few details. 'Effie'–it was hard for Barton to think of her as other than Agnes—had beautiful red hair, which Judith had envied. She had a quick eye and a quicker mind. She had a dapper hand at embroidery— just look at that handkerchief pattern. She'd been engaged, too, but the young man had resigned his hopes and married elsewhere after she'd been missing for months. Barton was going to ask more about the young man, when the mother returned with Jamie, the youngest of the four children. He looked to be about ten years old.

He rushed up to Barton with a look of excitement to ask, "You know where Effie is? Please tell us; I've been wondering why she doesn't write."

"Well, we don't know where she is, exactly, but we might have had a hint. That's all. Sorry to disappoint you," he said. The lad's face fell and he looked down. "It's all right," he mumbled, and disappeared from the room. And that was all he managed out of the visit.

Quite a tale of woe for this young woman, he thought. It did seem extraordinary that Sergeant Ragby had told her about her family connections discovered during the Tunbridge interview and that she would not have returned, especially if she was as loved and admired as they intimated. Unless Ragby had not told her...

Ever since Ragby had told him to report field observations solely to him, Barton had had a queer feeling about the man. Barton was not above suspecting the sergeant of making a play for his own ends.

A strange circumstance had him questioning the standing of this Worley character as well. What type of man came to holiday with his wife and retinue, only to leave every day to meet with his lawyer, in the nearest town, eight miles off? Barton stayed in the town and therefore observed Worley descend from his carriage at the lawyer's office each morning at eleven o'clock, confer with the solicitor inside briefly, and then depart.

Gerard Barton had many questions.

* * *

Agnes was in no way perturbed by any of these goings-on. She felt something like happiness, tending to her lady's maid duties, settling in with the staff closest to the family and learning about their history. After the ball, she had ventured to ask the Dowager Baronesses' housekeeper about how the couple had met and married.

"Oh, 'twas a love match, to be sure, my young miss." Mrs. Rose had nothing like the austerity of Mrs. Kingsley, and warmly recounted the well-worn story of how Sir Hereford and Lady Helen had met.

"She saw him in the circles at Bath when she was quite young and had taken no notice. So young, not even thinking of the men, can you think?" she tut-tutted a moment with good-natured tolerance. "But he had taken note of her, to be sure, even though she wasn't but fourteen years and he thirty. He spoke to her father and found good reception, but she being from such a good family, he felt he should have a bit more to offer, and so spent the next several years amassing a fortune, winning favors and connections in business, so as to be set up properly to provide for this young girl he'd fallen in love with."

Mrs. Rose sighed. "He returned to England from all his travels in Ireland, America, Canada, and Australia, and presented himself again to the family right here, courting my young lady fairly to win her affection." By now, Agnes was getting the feeling that some of this tale might have been embellished. "That he did, and with such tender attentions as Lady Helen didn't have a chance to resist. He showed himself to be respectable, refined—you know that worldly way gentlemen have of showing that they've seen such things in the world, and well, everyone was very satisfied."

Agnes weighed her next question: "Lady Helen never had any other suitors in the intervening time?"

Mrs. Rose rolled her eyes skyward, "La, of course she did, what do you think? The family so good in the neighborhood, and she a beauty? She had a dowry that was modest, of course, because of the entailment situation, but the suitors in those five year o' so, my, my!" Mrs. Rose's eyes shone.

"But her parents had told her of Mr. Worley's attentions and what he was doing in order to win her esteem, and it went a far way to winning her over with that!"

"I am glad they seem to like each other well even after much more time has passed," Agnes said, and continued in a lowered voice, "although it seems a pity there has been no indication of any children."

"Aye," Mrs. Rose sighed. "That I do not understand either, and we have not spared puzzling over it this many a year, when they do seem so happy with things as they are. None of us have any idea what will happen to the property if they both die with no issue. It is good enough to hope not to have to worry about it for a while, I suppose," she said, giving Agnes a wistful smile. "Now don't forget to clean the shoes before my lady retires. You'll know what she's to wear to church tomorrow."

Agnes realized with a warm feeling that she did know. Things were falling into an easy routine.

Chapter 37

Horace was away up north, riding God-knew-where to interrogate Devil-knew-whom. Henry meanwhile was pacing around the different rooms of his house, alternating between blood-boiling rage and the desire to curl into a ball and have someone else take care of this mess.

But there was no one else to take care of it.

His initial fear at the start of this whole disastrous affair, when he had discovered a naked woman in his bathroom, was that someone would attempt to blackmail his family, imputing the scandal of the crime to his family's good name, and the family business's good reputation, so that he would be blocked from investment ventures and denied entry to the gentlemen's clubs where so much of business was truly done. Now, it had happened, despite the temporary reprieve from worry that the police's secrecy had granted them.

Henry wondered why the blackmailer had waited the months until now to make his move.

Had he only found out? Hardly likely. It might be the group who had done this to Agnes in the first place: the hypnotizers. Had they been waiting on some contingency before playing their hand? Much more likely. But what had been the trigger? Was it something he or Horace had unearthed? Or, goodness, Agnes? Or was it just the police chain of command, not able to keep the lid tight on the case?

The priority at this point was to keep calm, to act as if nothing was wrong. They didn't want to alarm the servants or village people with whom the servants chattered. It was all such a house of straw.

While outwardly acting normally, Henry had tasked himself with devising contingency after contingency plan.

Horace was off trying to find the perpetrators, either the servant who had disappeared—and likely joined their household only to aid in this plot —or the original party who'd hypnotized and trained Agnes. Neither the MacFarlanes nor the police had yet had any luck tracking down either of these. And until his sleuthing brought to light any good leads, Henry must investigate ways to manage the police. Although Sergeant Ragby might or might not be part of this blackmail plot, the MacFarlanes would have to rely, or seem to rely, on him for discretion while they worked on a plausible alternative explanation to the one that might well leap to society's eyes from the front page: "Rail

Magnate's Son Seduces and Despoils Gentlewoman!"

* * *

Despite it being August, Scotland's reputed month of good weather, Horace seemed to have found the one wandering gale on the west coast, and it was howling about his ears as he trudged from his sparse lodgings at a village inn to the pub a few doors down. He had already discovered a significant piece of information on his blazing trip north. The first had been in a shady alley in Glasgow, cousin to previous shady alleys visited in Edinburgh, but this one much more likely to turn up a corpse the next morning.

Horace had wondered at his being there, blistering himself for getting into such a position moments before his contact arrived: a thin, twist-backed, black-faced man in his twenties or thirties, hard to tell. The contact had been arranged by one of his card sharp friends who knew people in criminal circles. This would be Horace's first foray in person into this world, and he had a momentary flicker of fear that he hadn't disguised himself enough. He brushed it aside. What's done is done, and had to be done, he said silently to himself.

"Crapper," he intoned, voicing the code name, or street name, of the unfortunate twisted individual several yards away from him.

"Aye," the man replied. Then silence but for

the wind.

Horace tried again. "I want information on two bastards. One kidnappin' an' one blackmailin'."

More silence.

"Names I have are Klein, Simpson, Lewes, and Turnowsky, that are involved in either one or both. Got no more'n a week to get it."

Horace determined to wait before contributing more information. And was rewarded.

"Ya got coin to pay, now?" Crapper asked in a thin whining tone.

"Three pound for expenses, and more when you've shown me something under a week. I'll be at the inn." Horace pulled the three pounds in silver pence in a leather bag from his coat and eyed this Crapper, waiting.

"Plenty to be shown, those bastards," he spat, "but what kidnappin' and blackmailin', 'at's the question."

"Kidnapping a girl from Glasgow in the last two years, hypnotizing her and dropping her into a gentleman's house naked and with no memory. Set-up," Horace spat back, tossing the bag at the low-life, thoroughly disheartened and disgusted. He needed to get out of there.

He made his way back to the inn, trying not to flinch at the street noises. The railway line enquiries seemed to go nowhere, and he hadn't much hope this fool's errand would either. The names he'd gotten from Kincaid were little more than a stab in the dark.

He was so fed up with this hiding from worry and fear; much better when he could hide out of spite, when it was just a gentlemanly debt or whispered word of reproached honor that kept him away from someone's company, not all company.

He was weary already of the distasteful nature of the underworld. He longed to ride back to the gamekeeper's cottage and see if that lead took them anywhere. And so, when he was warmed again at the inn, he sat down to some port that the inn had on hand and mused on Alice's pretty face as he remembered it, instead of the unseemly world outside his door.

He thought about that name Alice, belonging to an early, and what he had thought innocent, love. His mind ground over and over the feeling of something pure being taken from him and tainted, when he was most in need of something pure to restore him mentally.

Could she have already had an affair with his father before they had met, young lovers almost ten years ago? That was so incongruous with both his image of his father and that of Alice that he dismissed it as impossible and racked his brain for other explanations. Doing the math, she would have to given birth at seven or eight years old to be

Agnes' mother: clearly impossible. The whole insinuation made no sense!

Horace felt a bloom of confidence in his judgement again and stood suddenly, his thoughts turning to the journey waiting for him back on the family property to the northern border where the gamekeeper's cottage was. But at that moment, a knock sounded on his roughened inn-room door, and he sat back down, adopting a scowl and barking out a command: 'Enter!'

The innkeeper's serving-man opened the door and let in a cringing, down-at-the-mouth character, announcing, "A Mr. Ellers to see you, sir," before withdrawing and closing the door.

Horace MacFarlane stared at the man, who would not immediately meet his gaze, but slowly measured the room's contents and chose a chair by the fire, shrugging out of his dripping coat.

"I'm not sure we've been introduced," Horace stated drily, "But what might be your business with me?"

The interloper looked at him, then sat up straight, and fixed him with a considering look. He let his gaze fall back to the fire before speaking.

"You've spoken with a man named Crapper today," the man said in a soft, flat voice that surprised Horace with its base of gentility. "He is not the man you want to do business with. I am."

Horace let that sit for a moment in the tense

air, then asked a question.

"Can you tell me why that is so, or how you come to know what my business is, if indeed you do?

Ellers' eyes glanced up at him again before he emitted a small sigh. "You're asking a rat to rat on his business associates when you should be training a terrier to hunt them down." A pause. "Unfortunately, terriers are in rather short supply these days, and it is hard to be sure you have a good one."

Another pause, in which Horace's mind raced to assign roles of rat and dog to the various rat-like persons with whom he had had to deal in the past couple of days in and around Glasgow. He let his eyes wander over the man's face as he considered his words: a long face with a strong chin, a slightly crooked nose, and clear, dark eyes. They were trained now on him, staring coolly back.

"In case you haven't worked it out, I am classing myself as a terrier, unlikely as that may seem at the present moment." The shadow of a smile briefly crossed his features.

"I have been working with Her Majesty's Government," he said in a voice pitched even lower, "to unearth a plot of the direst kind involving people in this country acting to make alliances with certain unsavory movements on the Continent. That is all I will say. I am currently investigating a ring of spies who are trying to blackmail people in positions of importance in order to gain influence over certain political appointments. And you are one of the people. Or rather, your brother is."

That slight cut had stung, but Horace let it glance off as his mind digested the information he had heard, registering the implications and what it meant for the potential success of his mission to keep the whole story hidden from public view.

"And do you intend to solve these cases of blackmail through revealing the news and so robbing them of their power, or finding the blackguards and foiling their plan?"

Ellers nodded faintly. "Of course we are trying for the latter, Mr.—Johnston, is it? Yes, we are aiming for that, but you will agree it is more in Her Majesty's interest to save an ally-country from certain degradation than it is to save one high-ranking family some loss of social standing. I am sure your house would survive if it came to that."

He continued, ignoring the sudden paling of Horace's face. "At present, that is what I know of the plot that I can reveal. Is there more that you would like to tell me, sir?"

Horace struggled for a moment, the desire to throttle something reined in by his need for information and cooperation from this seemingly callous man with no regard for family honour. What else had one in Britain? Money would run out,

children would go their own way ... Horace realized he sounded like his brother. That thought
brought him back to the present decision: how
much to relay, and how much to trust?

"My brother and I have been investigating as
well, as you may have noted," he began slowly,
"and discovered that there was hypnotism involved
in the plot against us." He kept his eyes fixed on
Ellers to observe his reaction, but the man was
certainly a practiced professional at this sort of
dealing and betrayed nothing. "I am on an errand
now to find information concerning some people
we believe may have an interest in blackening our
name. I have not yet connected the motives to the
implementation, but that was my intent in coming
here."

"Bravely done, but I do believe you won't
get much out of that Crapper fellow. As I said, a rat.
I've given you the basic motive for the large affair,
but you don't believe that is the true motive for
choosing your family?" Ellers asked, as if merely
curious.

"No-o-o, not entirely. There are certain
points upon which my family is sensitive, and it
seemed to land on those too precisely for an international operative to be throwing the dart—"

"Ah, but they are a strange network of fellows—and ladies—this network. Fanatical and
motivated, and entirely willing to sacrifice years to

gain their position. You might be surprised."

"You may be right, but we would prefer to rule out more parochial possibilities first. Since you are examining the more global ones, perhaps we have a chance for mutual benefit here."

"Perhaps. You have until when— September? End of August?"

"September first."

"Then I would advise you to return home and monitor your neighborhood and contacts from there, especially any who seem more interested in your affairs than normal. And don't rule out the women in the network. You do so at your peril, for they are just as fanatical. Have you satisfied yourself that it is not the girl herself who is 'in it'?"

Horace tried not to show his astonishment at Ellers' knowledge of their secret. "My brother thought he had. I will see for myself."

"She is being shadowed by so many scores of witnesses that it is difficult to assign them each their patron, but it shall be done. One more thing: you, or your brother, is wise in choosing not to trust all the police. You might return to that line of inquiry, once home."

Horace looked at the gentleman again, seeing past the rakish black hair and soiled black collar, seeing someone thoroughly in charge, someone who did his business with a clear conscience. Something in his chest lifted, thinking of it, even though he didn't know whether or not to hope for better results in his own case.

"Sir," Horace rose and bowed, thanking Ellers with his outstretched hand and forthright gaze. They shook, and Ellers departed, the other wondering when he might reappear.

Chapter 38

"I honestly don't know what it was, but there was something in his presence and bearing that seemed upstanding," Horace was saying to his brother, back in Tidewater. "I do think we should call up your man on Agnes to see what she's been doing. Other than that, I will return to Glasgow in two days' time to see what information we have on any of those names that Kincaid put forward. I shall explore them all. I intend to—" he stopped abruptly, "Henry, are you even listening to me?"

"Yes, go on. I'm listening."

"I intend to find out where those men are whose names I passed on to Crapper. If he gives me any leads on that, so much the better. I will not go to the police with anything until I am quite sure of some connection to our foul affair and in possession of some proof that does not damn us in the process. I'll also do some backroom research in town on the political problems on the Continent, which Ellers hinted at. I say, Henry, why do you not respond? Are you well?"

"Perfectly well. In fine fettle. Just—shocked. Shocked, all over again. While you have been away, I have been doing my own digging here at home. I have made two significant discoveries, I think. Are you ready to hear them, now that you have reported out yourself?"

"Yes, of course."

"First, I wanted to pinpoint what had gone on at the warden's cottage, and I knew it was not a job for you, being so close to... matters in the case. I had Arthur question the cook's helper, a very old woman who knows the whole history of the place, she would say. And we have been confused, dear brother, which is good for your sake." Henry looked at Horace's puzzled and expectant, hopeful face.

"The game warden, a John Denny, who died five years or so ago of flux, and has not been re-placed—he had two wives. The first, a Mary Ellen from the neighboring village, bore him one son, Jeremiah. She died in 1873 from the pox. Two years later, John Denny married again, this time to an Alice," here he paused for emphasis, "Moore from Cambuslang. This second wife had the baby Jeremiah as a stepchild from a young age, and now she looks after him as her own. As for the relations with members of our family—"

Horace interrupted, "So then there is the key

to the mystery, which absolves me of my former worry and disgust over choosing the same mistress as my father. She was—only mine," Horace said self-consciously. "I am glad you had a chance to piece the history together. Thank you, Henry."

Henry nodded slowly, steepling his hands and keeping his head bowed in thought as he sat in the great fauteuil-chair of his father.

"Yes. And no thought for poor old John Denny, cuckolded twice, with two different wives, by his benevolent masters?" Henry sighed at Horace's shrug, letting the matter go.

"I had an interview with Mrs. Denny, Mrs. Alice Denny, to ask her about the money situation. It seems she had neither heard of the drama our houseguest caused nor seen the young amnesiac; thus, evidence of the two ever knowing each other is still missing. The woman seems quiet and willing to spend all her days as a stepmother living in that cottage with no society, so … we will leave that alone." A deliberate pause.

"The second discovery," he began at length, drawing out the words, "has to do with the girl—"

"Have you discovered who she is connected to? You may have thought her a pawn, but I am quite willing to believe she's a fanatic. When I—"

"HORACE." A stunned pause.

"If you will allow me to finish: the discovery involves the girl, her new employer, and the police sergeant Ragby. Now, I have not yet decided how much of this news to believe, just as you should not be so quick to believe all the theories this man Ellers has put before you." Henry quelled a restive movement of his brother's with a glance, which annoyed Horace to no end.

"Only this morning, a few hours before you returned, I heard from our spy Wendell, the policeman following Agnes in Leeds. Nothing out of the ordinary, he said, they are nearing the end of their stay at a family estate near the village of High Bentham before returning to Leeds in a fortnight. Take a guess where High Bentham is, Horace?"

"Not the faintest idea. Sounds northern."

"It is. But it also has direct access to the main road to both Stanraer and Portpatrick, making it a day's ride and a ferry away from Belfast, which plays into your rather grand notions of spy movements and all that. What is more, Private Wendell has heard from the Cumbria police department that Sir Worley, Agnes' employer, has been to see the telegraph office in Minnigaff every day that they have been in the country. Nervously. It looks to me as if this Sir Worley who hired Agnes is waiting to hear some important information... and may not be unconnected to the whole muddy affair after all— listen to this, Horace. Worley has an acquaintance with Sergeant Ragby; they were seen weeks ago by Wendell, breakfasting near Worley's club in Leeds.

"Furthermore, according to Fred our groom, Ragby has been keeping that Constable Norris from this case, instead pushing forward an out-of-town detective, with no local connections, to do all the investigating, which I would guess includes us."

Horace had tilted his head back as Henry spun the tale, trying to see the whole picture above him on the Georgian ceiling.

The wheels were still turning in his head as he asked, "So all the various people following Agnes suspect Worley, and your man on Ragby, that is, Fred, suspects him, and so you've leapt to join them in league together? I'm sorry, Henry, I don't make the same leap with Ragby and Worley. I still think Ellers' warning about fanatical women ought to be heeded. We should look more closely at Agnes herself. You did not feel his presence. He is most definitely on the right side."

"Horace, you yourself said that he would not hesitate to sacrifice our family's name for the country's political interests! What may be the right side for the country and what is best for us are not necessarily the same, as much as we hope it to be so."

"Yes, but I just don't... why don't we each follow our own leads and see where they take us? They are both plausible explanations, and we only have a few weeks left to pursue all possibilities to find our blackmailers. Maybe they are even connected. It is hard to know."

"And I do hate not knowing," Henry admitted. "You are right, Horace. You follow your bead on Agnes, only … tread carefully. You did not feel her presence that morning." A slight tremor passed through Henry's face at the memory. "I may have entertained feelings for her for a moment, but…" Horace narrowed his eyes at his brother. "But it has changed. She doesn't need that now anyway; she needs safety, and time. So I will follow Ragby and Worley's acquaintance and that trouble-making hypnotist Tunbridge. He's bound to know something, but how to find him and have it out?"

Horace smiled. "I'm sure you'll think of something, brother."

Chapter 39

Detective Barton was no further along in his quest to demystify Sir Worley's comings and goings. Having observed them for almost two weeks, with no change, Barton was beginning to think of visiting the house for a change, when there was an alteration in routine. Worley entered the solicitor's office as usual, but left with a folded document in his hand and a frown of concentration wrinkling his tall forehead.

Barton followed the man all the way back to the estate house on his horse, making sure the carriage did not make any stops and trying to keep a low profile himself. He dismounted his horse and led it to the nearby lake shore, acting like a visitor to the area out for a ride. He was contemplating a ruse to gain entry to the house and find the document when he heard the carriage coming down the drive again. He crested the ridge to see which way it would turn, and was perplexed to see it turn west toward him, back the way they had both just come.

As it was August and had been warm and dry for over a week, the carriage raised a substantial amount of dust as it drove back towards town. Barton hopped back on his horse and followed the carriage at a lengthy distance. Surely he could follow its direction by the dust cloud, since there was no one else on the road.

When he reached the crossroads indicating the turn for the town with the solicitor, he realized that the carriage had continued on west instead of turning off south for Minnigaff. Considering this, Barton paused. He wasn't going to follow Worley anywhere he might be seen and identified, since that would prevent future monitoring. Maybe he could find that document at the house, though, while it was occupied only by Lady Helen, her sisters-in-law, and the servants. He turned smartly and hurried his horse back in that direction.

* * *

Agnes grimaced. Attending church in August made for some difficult stains. The heat, the finery: it was lucky that they did not all faint from how much they perspired, she thought. She was soaking and brushing some of Lady Helen's finer gowns when she looked out the window and saw a man walking his horse across the front lawn. Robert, the Dowager Baronesses' groomsman, was walking forward to meet him. They conferred briefly, Robert pointing to the house, and the other man tipping his hat, handing off his horse, and continuing.

Agnes wondered at that. Her ladyship had not advised her of any visits, and surely if the two sisters were having a visitor, Lady Helen would have been invited to attend. Instead, Miss Eliza was in her salon writing letters, Miss Paulina was in the library searching for a new novel, and Lady Helen was on the other side of the house, playing the piano. She had better go down and inform her of the visitor so that the ladies might receive him.

Agnes took another look to be able to describe him. In his black suit he looked tall, with wide shoulders. His figure had a confident posture, but he was altogether too casual in bearing to be a gentleman, was her thought. Perhaps he had come about some of the improvements on the estate? She wondered who it might be; at that moment he looked toward the window where she was standing and caught her glance in passing. She quickly stepped back, hurrying to inform the missus.

Instead of conferring with the her sisters, Lady Helen flapped a hand at Agnes and told her to ask the purpose of the visit. Since it was not anticipated, neither she nor they could be expected to be available, and she preferred not to be so. Agnes went to ask the caller's name and purpose.

The butler had let him enter but left him standing in the hallway while delivering his card.

Agnes intercepted the butler and said Lady Helen had delegated the visitor to her. She took the card, which read, "Gerard P. Barton, Her Majesty's Service, Police Detective."

When she saw that word "Police," her hands shook visibly. Not here for the Worleys, she thought. Here for me. And when I thought I'd managed to forget it all and find a new life. Well, I have done that; now it's down to facing that unknown behind me. We will see if this Gerard P. Barton knows any more than I do.

* * *

After admiring the large gilt-framed painting of a hunting scene in the hallway, Barton sensed a presence. He turned and found the face he had seen examining him from the window. He was fairly certain she knew he was here for her case, by her steely look, but wasn't sure whether he should continue the ruse or just come clean. The question was, would she help him solve her own case?

"Good morning, Mr. Barton. May I ask what is the purpose of your visit?"

"Good morning, miss. I was interested in seeing Sir Worley on some matters of police business."

"I'm afraid you have missed him, sir. He departed not half an hour ago in the carriage, and we expect him to be gone for some time."

"Well, thank you for that news. I wasn't sure

if it was his carriage I had seen, but you have confirmed it. I wonder if you might be able to help me
with this matter, Miss—?"

"That depends, sir." She turned on him a
piercing look. "What do you want to know, and
why do you want to know it?"

Chapter 40

She was keeping him at arm's length, and Barton couldn't blame her. His first impression was that her sister Judith had been right about the hair but hadn't said enough about how lovely she was in general. Fair skin, neat figure, lively features. He made a mental note not to let her attractiveness skew his judgement. She had invited him to sit in the back parlor and was looking at him like he was an enemy cobra and she a mongoose getting ready to strike. So much for the ruse. But what could she know about him already?

"What investigation are you conducting, sir?" she asked.

"Well, miss, I am working with Sergeant Ragby,"—at this he noticed her eyes tighten—"to solve the mystery of where you came from and why you were abducted and your memory lost. I am looking into several angles, some of which could benefit from hearing from yourself, and some from Sir Worley, so I came here."

"I see. And have you learned anything that could be of value to me yet?"

"Miss—Broderick, is it? Yes, well, I'm sure you know it's impossible for police to divulge details of a case that may endanger further research into the case. I couldn't say what possible discoveries I had made until I was sure they were true and verified, or I would be spreading falsehoods, and a very bad detective at that." My goodness, but I am having to play this like a novice. Surely she deserves more than that.

Barton followed in a lower tone, "I have questions about some suspicious actions of Sir Worley's, for example, which could come to naught. And," he hitched a big breath, "I have some concerns about Sergeant Ragby's behavior as well, which I only tell you to suggest where the directions are pointing so far. This is where I am breaking with the police code and trying to be a good detective, police or no, and solve this case."

He paused to look at the carpet while she absorbed this bombshell, and hoped he'd gone the right way with this. Her change of tone told him he had.

"Detective Barton, I thank you for confiding in me. This coincides with my own suspicions about the sergeant, but Sir Worley having a part in it quite bewilders me." He looked up at this point and found steady, determined, and curious eyes on him. They searched for his sincerity.

"Miss Broderick, they are the only leads I have at the moment, so I'll have to follow them. They may merely direct me to a different path. One of the reasons it has been difficult to determine who is on the right side here is that a fair number of people are interested in what happens to you, for no clear reason. So I am trying to establish reasons. Do you know that there are at least three parties having you followed and observed these past weeks?"

"What?" she gasped, astonished. "Truly? Who—who is following me? I haven't noticed anyone... and here? In High Bentham? They can't have."

"I believe they have. One group is the police. The two others I have identified are likely not police. I believe one may be from the MacFarlanes. Do you know why they'd be monitoring your whereabouts?" he asked, as she gasped again at the mention of that family.

"No! I—I've no idea. It certainly doesn't make me feel better that they are..." She stopped herself abruptly, reining in her physical response, the heartbeat meter of which he could see pounding frantically below her ear. She subsided into momentary internal consideration. "Who is the last group?" she said at last, turning her face back to Barton.

And there's that quick mind.

"I don't know. They haven't used the same fellow, unlike the man sent by the MacFarlanes, so they've been harder to trace. But the house here is rather remote, which is helpful, since everyone will notice someone leaving your drive in the direction of the train. The two fellows in the unknown group have both left the area for Glasgow; I have not been able to determine further than that."

He could tell her mind was working furiously trying to connect the pieces of his information with any she might have at her fingertips. Her astonishment at the MacFarlane conjecture had faded, but she was not going to forget the Sergeant Ragby piece so quickly.

"That is a good deal more than I ever heard from the police in Carknocke County, Mr. Barton, so I do appreciate your telling me. I am sorry I cannot add to your findings. I'm sure you've already heard I am supposed to have been brought up in Glasgow," she stated, getting confirmation with a glance at his face. "Though I don't know any more than that, as far as a connection with people from there who may be f-following me." She paused. "I thought it was over. I thought if I just ignored the police long enough I could carry on with a new life and be happy—enough." She turned on Barton a look of such weariness that he moved his hand to his chest, feeling a pressure building there. This young woman was so expressive; he couldn't consider this an act. He couldn't.

She returned to the subject of her employer and his sergeant. "What have you found that makes you question Sir Worley or Sergeant Ragby, since you don't think any of the spies have their orders from either of them?"

"I didn't say exactly that. Ragby has me as well as another assigned to you. The other is not doing a very good job of it, but that may be intentional, and he may not want me to be doing a thorough job, either. I know that sounds terrible, but let me explain why I think this." And he explained to Agnes the shift in responsibilities from Norris to him, the lack of support since he had traveled away from Goole and the area in which she had been discovered, the suspicious non-investigation of certain contacts. It made him uneasy, and this was why he had wanted so much to meet her himself and establish more facts of the case from her point of view. So much he told her, before she asked again about Worley.

"Sir Worley. While I have been in the High Bentham neighborhood, I observed him coming and going to the village of Minnigaff at precisely the same time each day. Seeing where he went, I found it was a notary and telegraph office. He never stays longer than a few minutes. He may have left again to do just that, or perhaps some other errand… These visits seem to indicate he is waiting for something to come to him, whether information or money, something. Is there anything you know of, being in his household, that would have him doing this?"

"No, but we don't know much about Sir Worley's public affairs. I've more to do with Lady Helen and her social appearances," she said, shaking her head at the implications. "Well, I will certainly be more aware and attentive to whom I can see on my errands, with this news. Again, I thank you for coming and sharing your discoveries. I had resolved to repel any policeman that came to me with more inquiries that I couldn't answer, so I am glad you have come to give, as well as receive, news," she said, rising.

Barton marveled at her self-possession, wishing that they could converse about something else so that he could see how she acted in more normal circumstances. He accompanied her to the front door and asked how she liked the countryside.

"It is… it soothes my mind. I had thought it very restful, despite the moments that still intrude on me. But I'm afraid it will be hard to obtain that peacefulness again, now that I know there are spies 'round the place," she said.

"I've only been in this forest once, as a boy, and I loved it. I was up with my father to meet a relative coming in from Antrim once, and we spent the day climbing about and following the water. I thought it high adventure as a boy, but I also remember the calm. I hope it will still be there for you," Barton finished, looking up to meet her eyes, which followed him.

She was beaming her quiet gratitude at him, and his own troubled heart lifted. Agnes opened her mouth to say something, but he waved her off and promised to be back as soon as he had found out more. Barton was reluctant to leave her but now wanted even more earnestly to solve the case, and not merely for the promotion to the city post.

He urged her to be careful, and they parted.

* * *

Henry had spent a fruitless day chasing the spectre of Dr. Tunbridge at the University of Grantham. The man had been a professor in the Faculty of Sciences but had apparently left the previous year due to a disagreement of philosophy. His assistant, a Mr. Stemper, could not be located either. The department secretary had been none too pleased at being called upon unexpectedly outside of his normal business week and was therefore tight-lipped about where certain students might be found on a Saturday.

Henry wasn't sure whether to keep quiet about the urgency and rely on people being helpful or simply start relying on lies to make the situation appear urgent for a reason far different from his own private motivation. At the next interview, he decided to jump into the latter camp.

Without his valet, he was resorting to knocking on doors of the university's employee housing. At the next door, he discovered the university's provost, a well-dressed man of middling height and the long-suffering look of someone who thought himself important but unappreciated. Perfect, Henry thought.

"Hello, sir. So sorry to bother you on this day of leisure, but I am terribly worried about a friend whose sister was mixed up with some students of a Dr. Tunbridge. I—"

"Yes, yes, I know Dr. Tunbridge's history. He's no longer here, thank goodness, but that doesn't stop his power to make mischief. What happened to your friend? What's his name, then?" he said, clearing his throat and inviting Henry in to the drawing room with a sweep of his hand.

Henry learned more than he'd bargained for in the next half-hour: Tunbridge had held his post at the university for almost two years, teaching two courses at Grantham following a study mission in St. Petersburg that had won him some acclaim in 'scientific spirituality' circles. He had published a paper on the topic and held salons in addition to his formal classes for those interested in the subject.

The students attending the salons had all been men except for a few. One of the women was a sister of one of the matriculating students, and she was interested in neurology. Apparently, a month before Tunbridge's dismissal, something had happened during one of the salons that troubled the attendees, and it had involved the hypnotism of this same woman. After interviews with the young woman and her brother, Tunbridge had been dismissed for misconduct.

Henry took all this in, trying to maintain his part of a concerned friend for the young man when he was feeling a violent need to find this Tunbridge and strangle him for Agnes' sake. It was a very plausible explanation for what must have happened to her.

Henry spoke as the man paused for a sip of tea: "Thank you for explaining the situation to me clearly, sir. I think Tunbridge has done this same type of trick in more than one position and I hope he is barred from ever holding the post of a man of science again! You've done right dismissing him, of course. I just hope he isn't somewhere right now repeating the same scene. Perhaps if I talked to some of the students involved?" Henry asked, trying to make it seem a legitimate, spontaneous request.

The ploy worked, and he was given three names, all of which might be found at this hour on a Saturday of the summer term at the Iron Wing pub on Lowe street. Thanking the man floridly,

Henry stepped out, ready for this next battle.

Chapter 41

As Henry was knocking on doors in Grantham, Horace was passing through the village of High Bentham in his carriage. Since it wouldn't do for him to be seen visiting a servant of a high-born family one did not know socially, Horace had crafted a ruse to see Miss Broderick. He installed his few things at an inn in the nearby town, left his groom and valet, and set off walking across the fields to the estate at Clatteringshaws.

It was not an ingenious plan, and as he walked, he crossed his fingers that he wouldn't be observed by anyone who would recognize him, in disguise or no.

For in disguise he was: dressed in roughed-up, patched-but-clean trousers and shirt, he meant to look the part of a working man, dressed up to call on a "lady friend." He timed his visit to be well after the lunching hour, and he hoped that the occupants of the estate would be out visiting or retired, unlikely to notice a servant's visitor. Especially Sir

Worley, given Henry's news of his possible guilt.

He was impressed by the intricately tooled designs in the stone façade of the estate but didn't pause long on the path before skirting round to find the side entrance for the lower callers. At his knock, a uniformed woman answered immediately.

"Calling for Miss Broderick, please, for a walk. Tell her it's Horace." He tried to keep a minimum of words so his affected accent wouldn't sound quite so bizarre, and the woman let it pass without comment, eyeing him interestedly but leaving after a curt, 'Wait here.'

He waited. He waited several minutes, approaching a quarter of an hour, before he heard steps, and a white-faced Agnes stood in front of him, staring at him with only partially concealed fear. Their gaze held for a moment, then she dropped her eyes.

"Mr. MacFarlane, a walk around the park? Shall we be long?"

He tried again with the accent, in case they were overheard, "I don't think so, miss, but there's been an awful lot of news..."

She emitted a sound not unlike a contained sneeze when she heard him, still looking down, and had lost a bit of the fear in her eyes when she responded, "All right, then. Here we are," she said, indicating a path to the garden beyond.

They had walked a few minutes, putting

some distance between them and the house windows. Horace turned to her and spoke in his normal voice, which held an edge.

"Have you found out what happened and why you are here?"

Agnes looked at him queerly. "Is that what you've come here, in disguise, to ask me?"

"It is part of the reason. Have you?"

"No. But I am interested to learn why it is so important to you, gentleman of leisure that you are."

"Yes, I suppose our last meeting gave you that impression, that I am not very particular about my attentions. I do remember, however, that on that day you seemed to recognize me from before even though we'd never met. Would you care to explain that now?"

"I can't. I have recognized not another living soul from before this spring except yourself, and I've no idea why I should know you, as you didn't know me. Do you know now?"

"I have an idea."

There was a pause in the conversation, as Horace considered how best to push forward and get the information he needed, and Agnes felt less sure of herself and more afraid of what Horace's visit meant.

Horace resumed walking slowly toward the shady, wooded side of the garden. Agnes followed.

She cleared her throat, and asked, "Since I have no idea why I would recognize you, and you do, I would very much like to know what you think the reason may be."

"Because you were trained to bring me down in disgrace. Somehow. And that would leave my brother, on all his boards and committees and enterprises, vulnerable to blackmail to keep the family honor and industry intact. You, my dear, are part of a Continental anarchist fanatic group. What I am trying to determine is whether it was willing or not—"

"A contin—I? I can't believe this. It's ridiculous. How on earth—?"

"I am well-known for my dallying habits, unfortunately. You are a comely young lady. It is not out of the question. Also, you are employed by a man who has some very suspicious habits that resemble those of a blackmailer, habits which align nicely with the time period my brother and I started to be pinched in this whole affair. My family—you have involved our good name, and I cannot forgive it. I must know whether you are part of the plot too, and if so, how to stop it. It mustn't go forward. Henry would rather die than lose all that our father built up for us—"

As he loomed over her in the shade of the trees, Agnes saw a movement across the park from the direction of the road. Horace caught her glance and stopped mid-sentence, whirling to look in that direction. A man in a shabby black suit was hailing them as he came down the hill.

"Who is that?" he demanded.

Agnes' face was full of the swirling thoughts, conjectures, and horrors Horace had disturbed, and she could not immediately respond, as she tried to predict what a confrontation between Detective Barton and Horace MacFarlane would yield.

He leaned over her again, a full head above her, a keen gaze piercing her confusion.

"It's a policeman. He was here yesterday," she murmured, fear propelling the answer from her tongue.

"What for? What does he know?"

"I don't know, I don't know—he's trying to figure it out, too, everyone is trying to figure it out, except—" she pitched forward, feeling dizzy, grabbing onto a hedge for support, scratching her hand in the process.

"—Except me, everyone knows more than I do, about me… It can't be true. I'm not a bleeding anarchist—I'm not. I'm not!" she wheezed, then sucked in a big gasp of air.

Horace looked at the young woman, trying to pull back to an objective, rational perspective, but seeing again her position with Sir Worley, and what Ellers had implied. He remembered what his brother had told him to do: tread carefully. Too late for that, but he would try to ease out of it. He took Agnes' elbow to lead her to a stone bench near at hand when he heard the voice of the man approaching.

"What's going on here? I'm with the police. Stop, sir!"

Barton had been approaching the two of them, very curious about the visitor, but then as that visitor took a threatening stance and reached for Agnes' arm, he hurried to reach them and stop any intimidation.

He realized that the scruffily-dressed man leaning over Agnes was no criminal underling but a gentleman when he straightened and demonstrated the aplomb of a diplomat. His mind snapped the pieces together: the long face, the curly hair, the height, Agnes having admitted him for an interview —could this be Horace MacFarlane? Alarm bells went off in his head. It accorded with Ragby's description o him, but what on earth would bring him here in person, the dandy?

"I'm helping Miss Broderick sit down, that's all," said Horace, affecting his country accent again. "She's had a bit of a shock, but she'll be all right in a few minutes, won't you, miss?"

Agnes turned to them both, meeting Mac-Farlane's gaze, then Barton's.

"I have had a bit of a shock. But Mr. Mac-

Farlane—he is right." She walked the few steps to
the bench and the men followed, Barton offering
her his handkerchief to wipe the blood from the
cuts on her hand.

"Mr. MacFarlane thinks—yes, he knows
who you are—he thinks that I was drawn into an
anarchist plot and that is why I was hypnotized and
th-thrown on his family. Does that accord with the
leads you had, Detective Barton?" she said.

Barton was somewhat baffled. He had come
with news of Sir Worley and the police, but didn't
know what role the MacFarlanes played in the
affair. He decided to go along with Agnes' judgement, which he was inclined to trust after their last
interview.

"Miss Broderick, I can't say that I had
formed that hypothesis, but I'd be willing to hear it.
I do hope he knows you would be an entirely un-
willing participant in any kind of plot that may
have gone forward?"

"Detective Barton," Horace bit out, in his
normal register, "You will admit that someone
nervously, secretly, waiting on news during the
same period of time that we have been under
duress, shall we say, while employing the very
instrument of that duress, is rather suspect?"

"That may well be, but that says nothing
about the volition of the instrument—the person,
sir. Besides, that is what I have come with news

about today. Two points, sir: one, Sir Worley hired Agnes as a favor to Theodore Ragby, Sergeant Ragby's brother, and two, Sir Worley is indeed involved in blackmail, but on the receiving end of the stick, I'm afraid."

Agnes and Horace both dropped their jaws at this news.

Barton felt somewhat satisfied to have produced such an effect, after being disappointed in his effort to play the hero for Agnes.

"I don't know what to say," said Agnes, "I never would have imagined Sir Worley to be in such a position."

"I am in a position to appreciate how suddenly blackmail can occur, and to see that I may have been too quick to judge some factors of the case," said Horace.

"Might we find a place to sit and discuss this at more length, privately?"

They glanced at each other and around the garden, until Agnes nodded, and led them to an unoccupied greenhouse shed where they all sat at the pruning table to hear Barton's information.

Chapter 42

The Iron Wing Pub on Lowe Street was a generic establishment, hosting undergraduates of the university at their least intellectual moments. Henry MacFarlane stood out from the regulars by his age and refined carriage. He elected to make this work for him.

He asked the bartender about the three names he'd been given, and the man indicated a booth in a dark corner of the main room, where three young men sat eating their Saturday dinner.

Henry walked up to them and started on his newest-composed lie.

"I'm looking for the gentlemen Pye, Roydon, and Widdington? Yes, excuse me, gentlemen, but I am on a very urgent errand. It's about my daughter, and a man I believe you've had classes with, a Professor Tunbridge."

When he had mentioned a daughter, the eyes of some had registered concern, but when he said the name Tunbridge, they had all shown immediate alarm.

"Did your daughter attend classes with him here? I thought—well, the man's been run off, and good riddance, but I thought there had only been one woman attending here, and Miss Price is certainly back with her family now. Sorry, I'm Ron Widdington. Welcome, sir. Have a seat," he offered, moving aside.

"Thank you, sir," Henry said, joining them.

"Eliza is quite young but very smart. We live near Berwick, and I think she attended one of his lectures there. Do any of you know the topic? Or what he does, exactly? Eliza returned from the lecture almost a year ago and has become increasingly distant and dull, and I've heard alarming things when I ask about this man."

"Yes, sir, and so you should," said the young man across from Henry.

"Joseph Pye, sir," he said, shaking his hand. He continued, "What he does is hypnotize people. He makes them do things they wouldn't do in real life to demonstrate his control. I've heard of these things in other circles as well, but I thought we were getting 'round to the spiritualist part of the practice, to commune with the divine—I'm reading theology at university, thought it would be terribly exciting— but what he did instead was start rewriting people's memories. He would tell them it was Tuesday when it was Thursday, and when they were snapped out of it, they thought it was Tuesday. It began to seem harmful when he did that, and we started talking amongst ourselves about the indecency of it. That's when—well, Roydon will tell you. He was closest to the family."

Pye glanced to his left at the lowest-looking of the three— perhaps the result of recent alcoholism? thought Henry, who sat up a bit straighter.

"Aye. I was close to the family," said Roydon. "The family that was torn apart by that madman. I was good mates with Tim, who attended most of the same naturalism and philosophy courses I did. His sister Gwendolyn also had a scientific mind, and while she couldn't attend the University, as they haven't opened to women yet, she was allowed to come to lectures, and usually came with Tim to his.

"Tunbridge did the replacing memories bit Joseph told you about, as well as other bits, but he did it differently somehow, with Miss Price. It's like it found more fertile ground in her mind than the men's minds, and Tunbridge went too far in seeing what that meant. He basically experimented on us and on her, in front of all our eyes, and we didn't realize until too late!" Roydon had worked himself into an agitated state, but lapsed into sad reverie again, which Henry found easier to take, but still distressing.

"She went mad, knowing half reality and

half the lies he'd implanted. She—she suffers from it, as does Tim and the rest of the family... as do I," he finished quietly, hoarsely.

There was a stunned, respectful pause after Roydon's words.

"There's no way to undo the lies once implanted?" Henry asked.

"Not that we know of. Better to let the person live the one false life than tear their mind in two by living both the false and the true, awful as it seems," said Pye.

"Dear, dear. That is—this is distressing news. I am very sorry you've witnessed such an ordeal. Have you any notion of whether the professor escaped punishment, or where he might be now?"

Widdington said, "He was run out of this college, that's for sure. Don't know how many others would accept him, with that history, but maybe he's good at concealing it. He's probably very good at concealing things. We don't know where he went after here, sorry, sir... Best of luck with your daughter, sir."

Henry looked at them all, shook hands, and took his leave, distracted now with the thought that Agnes could be permanently damaged, irreversibly deranged. His blood raced to find that non-professor and wring his neck. He strode through the streets back to the station whence he had begun this charade, and bumped into another man who'd come lurching out from a side lane, propelled backwards by something.

He was yelling and shouting, leaning on Henry for momentary support, then ran back into the alley, presumably to resume battle.

Henry didn't care to view the alley scene, so focused was he on getting to the station and back home, but then bethought himself of the strangeness of the incident and checked his pockets —ah, wallet still there. But in the other, a scrap of folded paper that should not have been. He stopped. Should he read it now, before boarding the train, to make sure he got the message promptly? Or wait until he was on the train and in private?

He decided expediency was more important than privacy, and opened the paper on the sidewalk.

"H's Gl. research —> Rabilnikov: Brogan, MacRae, Brownlea, Surley, Madison

A's purpose —> Zemlya I Volya, Chatsworth, Berzinsh

E"

E? E-what? thought Henry. He would need a moment or more to puzzle out the message. He ran for the train.

Chapter 43

Horace MacFarlane left, and after assuring himself of Agnes' calmed state of mind, so did Detective Barton, leaving Agnes with their new tidings to consider as the Worleys spent their last few days at Clatteringshaws, this house and park which she had come to cling to as a safety beacon, far away from the rest of the world.

Two sides of her were at war. One wished to sweep all this turmoil and painful discovery under the rug and move forward through life as Agnes Broderick, lady's maid—Although hadn't I better find a new place, now that I know about Sir Worley's problems? She let that go for the moment.

The other side grasped desperately at the shreds of information relayed to her by others, just as it tried to do in the early days when she reacted to certain words or actions.

She tried to consider it logically: one side had low risk; the other, high. One side would cut out contact with unsavory characters; the other required it for a time. What if she looked into her past and found it to be terrible? What if she had more than a possible drunken father to be worried about? Could she stand that any better?

She did not know if she could trust her heart. And that discovery pushed her to dive into the past. She could not continue living this way; she resolved to confront any lurking demons before pursuing a new life.

Agnes was sitting in the greenhouse, thinking these things, when she realized it was almost time for dinner, and her mistress would likely be tardy, because of how late she was herself. She hurried to the house.

* * *

Henry was back in his own house, waiting for Horace to return from his investigative journey. He had guessed that the 'E' referred to the Ellers that Horace had met in Glasgow, further conjectured that the Gl meant Glasgow, and H referred to Horace, but the names all struck him as new; he hadn't the faintest idea what the second line was about, except that the Chatsworths were the Mac-Farlanes' main competitor on rail lines in the west of Scotland. He would ask his brother.

Or might he ask the police? Where else could he get credible information about a random tip? He knew that one of the names was Russian. Did he know anyone who knew about Russia? He checked his diary. Yes, his schoolfellow Ercolano was coming to pay a short visit, and he had studied music for some time in Russia. He might shed light on that part tomorrow afternoon. His diary also showed the date: August 23. One week.

Until then, Henry caught up on business correspondence, trying to let his mind rest after all the furious activity (and complicated lies) of his latest trip.

When Horace arrived home mid-morning the next day, he stomped immediately through the house to find Henry at his desk, lost in thought. Hearing someone enter, Henry turned to find his brother, hat and gloves still on. "Horace, what is it? Have you found anything?"

"I have."

"Agnes, is she—"

"She's out of it, brother. You were right."

Henry felt something settle in his gut, something he hadn't realized had been pushing against his lungs and chest. He let go a sigh.

"Well, there is a fair piece of news. Any more before I—"

"Yes, Henry. There was a man there, from the police, investigating and discussing some of his findings with Miss Broderick. Which he is not supposed to do, you may imagine. But it turns out this man, this Gerard Barton, has cast aspersions on the character of our good police sergeant, and believes he is somewhat implicated in this…business. This is the out-of-town detective that replaced that muck-about constable—the one we were worried about, you remember? Looks like he is on the good side as well," added Horace.

"Well," responded Henry, "and how is he getting on?"

Horace relayed the information about Ragby and Worley, and all the surveillance work that Barton had been doing. They decided that if Barton was going to be working with them, they could call off their less-than-eager tail, Wendell.

"And how did you get on, brother, with the Tunbridge lead?" Horace teased, feeling in better spirits than he had for weeks.

"Rather well, maybe even as well as you did. Tunbridge is all the scoundrel we expected, and nowhere to be found after being fired from his position for misconduct involving a method of intrusive brainwashing, which drove a girl mad who sat in one of his classes. Sound familiar?"

Henry continued without waiting for an answer. "Additionally, someone deliberately ran into me to set in my pocket a note. I believe it—well, let's see what you draw from it." Saying this, Henry picked up the note from his desk and handed it to Horace, who sat on the settee, and now thought to remove his hat and gloves.

He murmured the abbreviations to himself,

repeating the names and strange syllables several times.

"Yes, it is from Ellers, who used the same pseudonym to be recognized by me. But—ah! I know where they are from. These are names I found of the disappeared girls on the trains, when I was in Glasgow—the "G-L..."

As his voice drifted off, Henry spoke out, "Yes, I got almost as far. So now we see he has come to conclusions about our investigations and hands them to us on a silver platter! The disappearances, which were your 'research,' relate to the Russian name, which I don't think was on your list. And now I think the Chatsworths and the other two Russian names or phrases relate to 'A's purpose,' as in, why our girl Agnes is mixed up in this at all. How in bloody hell does he know all this?" Henry demanded, annoyed rather than angry that the investigations should seem so easy for someone else.

As Horace absorbed this, looking still at the note and reflecting on all the ins and outs involved, Henry continued, "I am waiting for my schoolfellow Piseo Ercolano to arrive in a few days for lunch, and we will delicately ask if he knows what any of these names and phrases mean. He is nothing if not discreet, despite his being Italian, and studied and traveled in Russia for several years."

Chapter 44

There was some confusing news.

Barton had not been able to search and re-cover the document that Sir Worley had deposited in the house that day, but he had observed another of his later trips to the telegraph office in Minnigaff, which resulted in the large man steam-ing out with a fierce expression on his face. He didn't carry anything with him, so Barton went inside to see if the telegraph employee might be of help.

With tact and lowered tones, the detective won him over. The employee described the source of the baronet's frustration to be a cable from Ab-erdeen, which he had promptly crumpled and tossed into the fire grate near the door, tossing in his own match while grumbling. There was nothing left of the cable. But a clue for their side: Aberdeen.

How did this square with Horace MacFar-lane's news of the blackmail letter, though? It might corroborate the theory that Worley was being blackmailed, but did it disprove the theory that he was also blackmailing someone else? No. Barton went to the big house, approaching the servants' entrance this time, and met with Agnes in the same back parlor as before.

He related to her his findings, urging her again to be careful. "What I can conclude from this is that you may be in a very tenuous position here, Miss Broderick," he said in a lowered voice.

"I believe you are right, Mr. Barton, but what else to do? If I leave now, I will never get another place as good. Perhaps if I ask for leave to visit family—"

"Yes, that might be the right idea. Have you wanted to?"

"Yes, of course! But what will I find? That is my worry."

"Miss Broderick, I must tell you now that I have been to see them, on the sergeant's orders, before I ever came here. I meant to tell you when I found out your feelings on the matter, but didn't have time before. There is no reason for you to worry. They would be very happy, I believe, to discover you alive—after being missing two years."

"Two years?"

He nodded.

She took a shaky breath. "That is longer than

I—I mean, not that I knew, but—two years is a substantial amount of time to explain, and I have no explanation."

"It won't matter to them. Trust me."

She looked at Barton and nodded. "Very well. We leave the day after tomorrow, and I will broach the subject with Lady Helen when we return to town. What will you do next? Follow me to Glasgow? Help me find them, at least?" She gave him a wry smile.

"It would be my pleasure."

* * *

Two days later, Barton followed the coach party of Sir Worley, Lady Helen, and their small entourage as it journeyed from High Bentham south to Leeds. He was aware of only one other tail this time, and it looked like one of the alternating fellows, but he couldn't be sure.

After his short, tense discussion alone with Horace MacFarlane, he knew he had not been completely taken into the confidence of the family, but he did feel as though his information was trusted. Small comfort. Having worked out that the situation involving Worley's vulnerability was tied to a certain speculation many years ago, he felt sure that now the only danger was from the hypnotist's corner. He still hadn't decided whether the band of ruffians had dropped Agnes permanently, or might return to put her under their power again.

He mused, and the journey continued, he comfortable on his horse and the coaches a good distance ahead. They stopped to sup and stay at a gracious inn at Clifton. Here, Barton bit his lip, wondering if the police force would cover the cost of a night there. He also wondered what Sir Worley would do, away from any telegraph office or telephone depot where he might receive word about his own purgatory.

He stabled his horse, gambling that the price would not be too outrageous here in the country. As he entered the common room, he noticed Sir Worley already at the bar, speaking to another gentleman with his back to Barton. There was a strangeness to Worley's manner, a gruff consternation, which Barton wanted to investigate.

Before he could, the valet that was traveling with them swept by him, mercifully not recognizing him even after his long interview at the house two days ago.

Good, Barton thought. We were not spotted together and examined: a narrow chance.

He followed the servant to the second level and saw the layout of larger rooms on the side facing the road, while smaller servants' rooms faced the back. Satisfied with knowledge of the building's layout, he returned downstairs, heading off any questions from an inn housekeeper by nodding decisively at her and brushing past.

He headed straight for the bar, where he found Sir Worley alone, looking troubled. Barton decided to make a direct appeal.

"Good even, sir," began Barton.

Worley's large head popped up from its downcast state, his eyes jumping to Barton's face.

"What? Yes, yes, good even to you,' he said, clearly distracted.

"I know this is hardly polite practice, but I am a detective with the police, sir, Detect—"

But Worley's eyes had snapped at once into an angry shape, "The police? Now why on earth—that is, how the devil—oh, Christ and his messengers! What have you to say to me?"

Barton knew that Worley would be wary of the police at this point, but had not wagered on his immediate blustery defensiveness. Had something happened? Had he gotten another telegraph and Barton had not noticed?

"Sir Worley, my name is—"

"Bugger what your name is! You have nothing of interest to say to me, I am sure. I am a respectable gentleman, and quite affronted at the presumption of introducing yourself—"

"Sir. I only want to talk to you about one of your servants. I am inves—"

Worley cut him off again, his whole being seeming to grow, puffed up and indignant.

"My servants?" his voice rose in pitch and

volume. "What on earth! If it is a question about the servants, you should wait until the household returns to Leeds and query the housekeeper, not bother me with such trifles, and while we are traveling! The nerve…I am telling the proprietor of this inn at once of your insidious presence and having you removed. Expediently." He signaled to the barman to do just that, took his drink, and whisked himself away toward the back verandah, still spluttering.

Detective Barton was quite astonished at this spectacle, but strove to quickly determine its cause before he was ejected from the place.

Defensive toward the police, yes, but seemingly not about the speculation rumors—odd. Maybe that man he had been talking to—yes, perhaps he had delivered an upsetting message, but concerning something other than the speculation business—

His thoughts were interrupted as the barman pointed to him, and he realized a short man was standing behind his seat, flanked by a large muscular man who looked like he threw horses for a living.

"Gentlemen, I am a police detective," Barton said. "Here is my badge."

He showed it to them; they looked at it with interest, and the short man asked in a long-suffering tone, without looking up from the badge, "Is it necessary to question my most high-profile guest in weeks within minutes of his arrival here, Detective?" Obviously they were in need of business.

"He'll be thinking I called you in a'purpose, which is quite unfair, and I'll have lost a chance for some renewed business," he paused. "If you could please wait in the front parlor, we will send a note up to the gentleman to see if he will speak with you after he is rested and restored to his own self," the man finished, with a slight Irish lilt.

Now Barton's suspicions were on higher alert. Repelled by Sir Worley, asked to wait downstairs by the hotelier, he sensed something was happening and he was being kept out of it, but had no idea what it could be or how he could intervene. Were Worley and this little man actually in league? It seemed implausible, and yet...

"Would it be all right if I stayed here at the bar to wait, then, sir?"

"Yes, that would be fine. I am content, and thank you for understanding that we must sometimes suffer the whims of our customers. You, no doubt, have had to do the same with investigations. I hope this one ends profitably." And with that strange choice of words, he left Barton at the bar, the common room now empty.

Not deigning to order a drink now that he was so vexed, Barton again racked his brain to deduce what he might be missing.

If only he knew the mission of the hypnotists, he might be able to connect the dots of the larger picture. All he could think of was Worley's past shady speculations being used for blackmail, but he must not be in danger of his actions becoming public any longer, if he had brushed off a policeman with such little care.

The man with whom Worley had been talking, however, had caused that worried look to appear on his face, then a dark, brooding look. Maybe he had just had to pay up for the blackmail? Or could—no—Barton jolted to his feet. Could he have been visited by someone in the gang of hypnotists who knew Worley's blackmailers and cut a deal?

Oh God, no, Barton thought as he sped away from the surprised bartender toward the back stair, please let that not be the case.

He pushed past the same housekeeper on the way up the stairs, making a good deal of noise. He went to the room he remembered Worley's valet exiting, and burst in: empty. He went to the next small bare room: nobody. The next held the groom, who was seated on his bed, polishing his boots.

The man looked up, alarmed at Barton's entrance, and then more so at his terrible expression. He stood.

"Sir?" he said uncertainly.

"Miss Broderick. Where is she?"

"Miss... why, she's resting in the next room, sir. What—"

"Which?" Barton demanded. The groom pointed one more room beyond, bewildered.

As Barton crashed out, he listened at the door a brief moment before entering: empty. There was a sweet, lingering smell that the detective recognized as chloroform.

"Damn!"

He stood a few moments in the doorway of the little room, trying to calm his thoughts and emotions, trying mightily to determine how best to stop the villains who must have just taken her. Finally, he felt a presence behind him; he turned to find Sir Worley himself, staring at him grimly.

Chapter 45

Piseo Ercolano turned out to be as little an example of Italian excess as one could imagine. He arrived at Tidewater driving his own small cabriolet, dressed in a dark grey wool worsted suit. He was stopping only for the afternoon, on his way to meet the parents of his hoped-for bride. He was in a fine mood then, with some added nervous energy, as he entered the hall and greeted Henry, and then Horace.

Henry said, "Well met, indeed, Piseo. Do let us have a walk in the fresh air before we sit down to lunch. We have a half-hour or more, as you have so excellently timed your entrance."

They exchanged some of the details of their business since they'd last met over a year ago, as Horace listened. Then Henry let his face exhibit complete seriousness as he invited his friend to sit in the arbor where they had arrived on their walk. They all sat.

"We've had a bit of trouble in fact lately, and

I was hoping you might shed some light on some information that has come our way. I believe it to be from someone trying to enlighten us as to the source of our troubles, but as I am completely unfamiliar with Russia and her current politics, I am quite at a loss to proceed further. Would you kindly consider whether you know any of the Russian names we've been given?" Henry asked.

He handed Piseo a sheet of new paper on which he had written only the two Russian names and the Russian phrase. No need to put other confusing information before his eyes.

As the small man read, his countenance blanched. He turned to Henry, put his hand on his arm, and said, "I sincerely hope you are not under the influence of Rabilnikov. He is the most famous of the criminal heads of state. He is either a good friend or a terrible enemy, so I hear."

He paused, his eyes returning to the page.

"As for Zemlya i volya, you have not heard here that it is they who were responsible for the assassination of Alexander II in '81?"

Horace looked up at that, muttering quickly, "No, but it fits."

Piseo let go that enigmatic comment and continued, "They have probably committed many more acts of anarchy than are generally acknowledged, but so many of their followers die in the act of blowing something up that it is hard to question them on motive at that point." He looked at the paper a final time and shrugged at the last name.

"This last is not familiar to me. I could only say that it sounds like a name from the northwest, near the Baltic Sea. There are many Berzinsh there."

A small pause ensued, which Henry broke after a few minutes of silent contemplation.

"Well, my friend, that will help us immensely in unraveling our mystery, I am sure. Now let us talk of other, more pleasant things, shall we?"

* * *

When lunch was done, cigars had been smoked, and Piseo Ercolano had been well wished on his way to his prospective in-laws', the brothers MacFarlane met in the library.

Without preamble, Horace outlined his speculations.

"We have a famous, and I will wager—sorry —I will presume, unforgiving Russian criminal behind the northern girls' disappearances. Perhaps that doesn't touch us at all, except that now the low-lifes know I was poking around looking for information on them. Damn."

"But we now have just the international movement Ellers was alluding to when he told me of the fanatics targeting people in positions of influence around Britain and the Continent—this Zemla ee-whatsit— I don't know if I want to know more about them. Their anarchist methods are sure to be—"

"Yes, they are sure to be terrible and distasteful and all the more reason for us to stop it from happening to us, Horace. And to that poor girl," Henry added.

"How can we know if the two are connected? It changes completely how and with whom we have to deal. If the mesmerists are the anarchists, and the blackmailers are the anarchists... Oh, and can we completely forget the police in all this? Are they in league with anybody?" Horace wondered aloud.

"And don't forget, Horace: that last name. Berzinsh. Who do we think that is, and how does it connect to the other pieces? Is it something connected to Agnes, or to the Chatsworths in the North?" The sound of his words dwindled as Henry felt the weight of too many possible endings to this story.

"I think it's time," Henry said, "to involve both Miss Broderick and that detective. He seems to be better at getting information, and she may have been able to put together the other pieces of this nasty business," he said. The frustration of the many long weeks of tension showed in his attitude of defeat. Horace came to his side, put an arm around his shoulders.

"Yes."

Chapter 46

Upon their meeting at the inn, Worley tried stonewalling Barton, aiming to send him away.

"She's not here any longer, and there's nothing you can do about it, young man. She's gone."

"You mean she has been taken by someone and you let it happen? I must find her. Agnes is in danger—"

"Ah, 'Agnes,' is it? I thought it was a bit quick for any of the policemen I know to be so close to the truth, but that explains it."

"It explains nothing, sir," said Barton, bristling. "I am a police detective, trying to solve a case of corruption and foul play. And you are most certainly in the center of it now. I'll be reporting this to Sergeant Ragby, as evidence points to—"

"To what exactly, Detective? A new servant leaving her employers on a whim?" Worley returned derisively. "I believe your sergeant, whoever he may be, will not take that as irrefutable evidence against a gentleman's word."

Barton glared at the rotund man, feeling the truth of those words. So Worley thought he knew his motives—well! It was true he had no way of detaining the man at present; his concern was all in overtaking whoever had kidnapped Miss Broderick. And the 'gentleman' would obviously not be helping.

"I'm sorry I cannot help you," Worley said, echoing Barton's thoughts, "but it is no longer my business and I can give you no more information." As he turned to go, he muttered clearly enough for Barton to hear, "she's with some hard ones now," before exiting the corridor.

Barton agonized over what to do next. He could think of no way to track the villain that had kidnapped Miss Broderick, as they must have gained at least twenty minutes' headstart and he had no thought of which direction they might have gone. He resolved to follow the Worleys home to make sure there was no further contact made, and try to find the thread of the hypnotist lead once again.

He prayed she was not lost to the cause already.

* * *

The Worley household returned to its house that evening in Leeds, and for some hours the servants unloaded and unpacked the trunks, groomsmen unhitched and put away horses and equipment, and gentle people rested from the tiring journey.

Lady Helen was in her rooms changing her dress for the evening meal. She was piqued to be told by the housekeeper that her lady's maid Agnes had had to leave on an errand as soon as she returned to Leeds. She would have to undress and choose her clothes with the help of the cook's assistant for the time being.

Mrs. Kingsley the housekeeper had told this to her mistress as it was passed on from one of the groomsman returning with the carriage, and she was fair vexed about it, too.

New girl, she thought, as hasn't earned her stripes yet, already taking her own leave, or obeying someone as isn't her superior. That certainly won't do in future. And she stewed about this while she helped put away the things in trunks.

The groomsman who had told Mrs. Kingsley had been told the news by Sir Worley's valet. Upon the carriage entering Quebec Street, the valet James had leapt down from the coach to tell John, the waiting groomsman, that they had had to let out Agnes at the last street for an errand. John was surprised, but relayed the information to Mrs. Kingsley, who would know how to handle such a hiccup in the running of things.

James, who had accompanied Sir Worley on the trip, was wearing a new waistcoat, in the pockets of which were placed not a few coins. As he helped his master down from the coach, they nodded at each other. The only thing left to ruin this perfect chain of lies was the man that jumped off his horse and followed Sir Worley nearly to his front door: Gerard P. Barton.

Chapter 47

When Barton arrived in Leeds, he found a vantage point to observe the Worley home in an alley across the street that housed an empty shoeshine stand. As he waited and watched, he composed several cryptic requests for assistance and information to colleagues in York, where he had been at school and had some personal connections that he might be able to use.

Barton requested information and leads on the character named Tunbridge, a known alias, from headquarters in London. He requested current information on the same from the professors at Grantham with whom he had already communicated. And he wrote to the MacFarlanes, warning them that the situation had turned very dire and that Miss Broderick had been kidnapped. All these scraps of paper he signed and sealed, then found a passing telegram boy to deliver them to the post office for sixpence, half again upon return.

He watched but the house gave no signs of

life. Calculating Worley's level of treachery, Barton figured he must have been blackmailed but grown used to it. That would account for his wealth at present as well as his increasingly sanguine entries into the crime world; he was drawn into it, had grown accustomed to the game, and now grew scornful of those who still tried to keep law and order.

He gathered that his wife knew nothing of his activities, hence the lie he saw passed through the servants. He would wager that the valet James had just been initiated into the circle of trust, based on his behavior.

Perhaps this valet could be a weak link, thought Barton. But then again, he might just as easily cling wildly to his new patron against all comers.

Barton considered appealing to his sergeant, but then realized it was likely that Ragby himself was funneling the information to Worley to blackmail the MacFarlanes. That would explain why he wasn't actively conducting the inquiries, and why he was avoiding the house in Tidewater altogether.

By the time the telegram boy returned, he was given another commission: food for supper. Barton ate the procured cold sliced mutton, bread, and cheese slowly, pursuing any leads he could remember, waiting for information to return to him. That night as he watched, he did anything that would distract him from thinking of what Agnes might be going through at that moment.

Chapter 48

Barton's letter, when it arrived in the Mac-Farlanes' hall, had nothing to do but wait, since both masters had left the previous day for Leeds.

They'd left to find Miss Broderick but were found instead by Barton who, after two nights of watching and receiving no answers to his urgent queries, was on the point of departing the alley when he caught sight of the two of them.

Henry and Horace MacFarlane were striding down the lane, having come on foot from their lodgings, procured near their target. The lane was a moderately busy one, neither commercial nor overly social, so their passage aroused interest but not comment. But Barton's detective eye, by now honed to sharpness, caught the familiar gait that he had observed back in High Bentham, and he hurried to intercept the men.

Horace saw him first. Knowing that three men in an alley would be noticed where one man was not, Barton signaled them to walk around the corner to a small public greenway. They all sat on a long bench, and the detective updated the brothers on what they had obviously not yet learnt. He did not know why they had come without first replying to his message, but he assumed that they would divulge any new information they might have so that they could all three work together.

The MacFarlanes, now possessing two leads, were not in agreement about this.

The younger MacFarlane, having first doubted the young policeman, now wished to include Barton in their confidence and pool their resources. The elder MacFarlane meanwhile gritted his teeth and glared at Horace to remain quiet, an anger at their situation boiling in his breast, taking aim at this police representative who was connected to the same Sergeant Ragby who'd mucked up the investigation and suspected Henry of having something to do with the plot.

When the pause after Barton's recitation had stretched uncomfortably long, Barton looked hard at Henry, feeling his resistance. Barton spread his hands upward in front of him, shrugging slightly.

"You're right that I won't care overmuch if you're hurt in this," he said. "My concern right now is for the woman who will be used for a nefarious purpose and tossed aside, when she deserves none of that. I hope that you can see that it is worth it to work together, Mr. MacFarlane."

Henry's glare directed itself to the ground now, and after a few seconds, the iron went out of him, his shoulders slumping, his head dropping a notch.

"Yes," he said simply. "There are things we will have to manage, if we have success in stopping this one madman, but they can wait until after. I am thinking of the sergeant, your boss. But they should not concern us now. Let me tell you what we have learned about our enemies."

Henry explained about the agent of the Crown surreptitiously giving them hints about the hypnotist Tunbridge being connected to the fanatical Russian anarchist movement whose members had assassinated Emperor Alexander the Second of Russia two years before. He also noted that the Chatsworths of Aberdeen were somehow implicated in this plot, and it was likely that their involvement had made the MacFarlane family the target for collateral damage. Finally, he revealed that they had done some research that might make them vulnerable to these Russian anarchists.

Another pause ensued in the low conversation among the trio of men in the public greenway. The detective had his head lowered, absorbing the information and connecting it with his own, trying to piece together a path forward.

"This is taking us into much wider circles than I had heretofore believed were involved in the

matter. Sir Worley's behavior at High Bentham
made me think that he was the orchestrator because
he seemed so much in control, but then, he must
have had plenty of time to perfect his dissembling,
if his blackmail has gone on as long as we think it
has.

"If Miss Broderick has been taken by the
same people," here Barton's voice caught up short,
and he cleared his throat. "The same people who
first abducted her, then it may be because she did
not serve her intended purpose, that of tainting your
family name and therefore your company. Since
nothing has surfaced, she has perhaps been put
back into training,"—his steady voice hiccoughed
again—"Or she's been disposed of. This has possibly already happened, as three full days have
passed. Do you have any information on where the
movement might be headquartered? The lack of
that knowledge is what has kept me here, when I
would much rather have followed the trail to the
vermins' nest," he said.

"I agree with your deductions, Detective,"
said Horace. "And I have been racking my brain for
some clues from the interviews we've had, but all I
have are the places that Tunbridge, or whatever his
real name is, has lectured: including Berwick, unless we want to try Aberdeen, based on Worley's
—"

"Yes," said Henry. "It's where Worley got

his upsetting telegram from; it's where the Chatsworths are headquartered. As good a place as any to start demanding answers."

"I could send messages to the police in a few of the other towns as well with Tunbridge's description and request any reports of wrongdoing connected with hypnotism," said Barton.

"I think our best bet is still one of the northern cities," said Horace. "They have the advantage of anonymity, convenient transportation both in Britain and across to the Continent."

"Shall we start in Aberdeen then, with the old cod?" Henry asked.

Horace shrugged. Barton gave a decisive nod. They all looked back toward the house on Quebec Street. Its windows were still covered with dark curtains.

Chapter 49

The next train they could catch was a sleeper that left Leeds late that evening, journeying through Newcastle to Aberdeen and ending in Wick. All three men boarded with nothing but the clothes on their back and the notes in their purse. Before the train sounded its whistle to depart, a porter ran through the cars, calling "Detective Barton, Detective!" Barton poked his head into the inner hallway to find the porter, who gave him a telegram.

It read:

HEAR GIRL IS GONE WITH BEAU STOP NO NEED FOR FURTHER SURVEIL STOP RETURN TO HULL FOR REASSIGN SGT RAGBY END

Barton read it through twice and stared at the ground, crumpling the paper in his hand. The MacFarlanes glanced at each other, and Henry asked, "Detective, what is the matter?"

Barton handed him the telegram in a crumpled ball. He said quietly, "I believe there has been some question in your mind about police involvement in the blackmail end of this affair, and this seems to provide some support for that theory. I would not have wanted to believe it, but…it will not stop me. I cannot stand by and let the police be used in such a way. Neither can I leave Miss Broderick to the mercies of this organization. They will not be kind. They—" he paused a moment. "They have not been kind, but she has persevered. Let us hope she has not persevered in vain. Let us hope we are still in time."

"Well, we did have suspicions, but this does seem to confirm that Ragby is under somebody's thumb, whether Worley's, or whoever has just stepped in above Worley," stated Horace.

At that moment the whistle sounded. The brothers looked at Barton, who still stood in the hallway, gazing out the window. The train pulled away; Barton entered the compartment again and sat down.

Chapter 50

As the train pulled into Aberdeen, Horace woke from his dozing; Barton opened his eyes from his considering pose; and Henry continued to sleep, until nudged awake by his brother. The Mac-Farlanes went to the hotel in town for accommodations.

It had been decided that the detective would be their guest. It was not very low-profile or clandestine of them, but as they would be going to consult with Old Man Chatsworth as themselves, they couldn't very well be in disguise anyway. Barton, who would not attend, could.

The attendant at the Chatsworth gate watched as two gentlemen approached. They introduced themselves briefly, and he dispatched an emissary to the office building just beyond. While the two men waited for the emissary's return, he returned to his primary duty of observing and noted that another shiftless character had joined the usual down-at-the-heels beggar across the way. He watched the pair idly, waiting to see the usual man assert rank and chase the other from his territory, but he was disappointed as the one just nodded to the other.

The emissary returned after ten minutes, whispered in the attendant's ear, and returned to his post inside the yard. The attendant related in diplomatic terms that Mr. Chatsworth was all booked with appointments that day and evening, but could see the MacFarlane gentlemen the next morning at ten o'clock. Henry let him see that he was a bit steamed at that, but thanked him and left civilly. Horace held his tongue.

"The nerve of the old man—why, he must know—he must know the matter which we intend to broach—" muttered Horace angrily as they walked stiffly away.

"Perhaps he does not know that a certain pawn is still in play, brother, and that there is urgency required. We let him know we are displeased. Let that lull him into arrogance for when we come tomorrow and place before him all we know. Then we shall see what he 'must know,'" replied Henry.

As the gentlemen were leaving the gate, the shiftless character, now spared the attendant's attention, flipped the beggar a coin, told him he'd return, and thanked him for his aid, slipping back into the alleys and shady corners of the city.

The trio reunited at the hotel. It was now noon, and they were all exhausted and starving after the journey and the tension of the morning's failed mission. Horace ordered some food from the hotel's club, but Barton immediately went to sleep. Henry teetered on the edge of drowsiness but decided to stay awake to eat before letting himself rest. Barton hadn't said anything, but Horace suspected the man would try something that night, so desperate he seemed to find Agnes.

The next move turned out to be a covert stop at the police station, also in disguise. Barton told the brothers of his plan during their brainstorming strategy session in the afternoon. He would leave a few hours after dark. He intended to speak with the deputy in charge and request replies to his letters, which he had directed to be sent on to Aberdeen, and then return to the hotel by one o'clock in the morning. The naps and food had helped a little, but without any new information, they didn't want to take any rash action before seeing Chatsworth. There was nothing for it but to wait.

When the brothers MacFarlane woke early the next morning, they saw no sign of the young detective.

Chapter 51

Detective Barton was not over-familiar with Aberdeen and, not wanting to become lost, he had made a beeline for the police station based on directions from the train attendant. Once there, he introduced himself to the constable on duty and asked after his letters.

"Haven't seen any pass through yet today, Detective. Reg'lar post comes before nine in the morning, if you'd like to check back then. Geordie'll be on b'that time," said the constable, an older gentleman with whitened hair and a squinty face.

"All right, thank you, sir. I shall. Now if you could also assist me with some local information…" and they continued to talk for half an hour about local roads, transportation, the Chatsworths, and the other high families in town.

One piece of news about a community investment plan financed by the Chatsworths caught Barton's attention. He replied in a curious but casual way, hoping not to appear too eager.

"You say they've cancelled the project? Any reason given?"

"Well, now, no reason given, as you say, but plenty of speculation, as well there might be. The family was in a way to make a lot of money from the rent on the property chosen but so were the people who lived alongside the property. Now that it will stay a wreck, those people are mighty disappointed about the Chatsworths promising a new hall and not deliverin'," he said. "And the speculations are mainly that the family has lost some money recently," the constable said quietly.

"That would fit, wouldn't it?" replied Barton. They sat in silence a few moments, each considering the abundance of motive if one looked. Barton said, "Well, I'm off now, be back in the morning to check the post. You've been very helpful, Constable. Do look me up if you're ever down Leeds way. I've no permanent place at the moment but will likely be there for some time. I'd be happy to repay this favor."

"Ah, 'twas nothing, sir. Glad to help. And I hope you find the person you're after, to be sure. Best of luck."

They shook hands and Barton left, but not for the hotel. It was only half past eleven, but as it was Aberdeen, city of industry and firm Presbyterians, everything was shuttered and few lights shone.

He made his way slowly to the dockside, approaching the quay where the country's herring poured in from the sea. He sat in the shadow cast by a tall gas lamp set on a pole. Several men were mending nets and talking amongst themselves.

He noticed the dilapidated ruin of a building a few hundred yards inland from the warehouse the fishermen were using. If it was the one discussed by the constable, it was indeed in a sad state; no wonder the fishing folk had been joyful at the improvements and new rooms proposed by the landlord. But did it have any significance for his case, he wondered, or was it just more city gossip?

It certainly fit that the Chatsworths had anticipated receiving money, made plans, and then when they did not receive the extortion money expected from the MacFarlanes, had to withdraw from the work they had planned for that money. Possible. But how would the connection between an otherwise respectable family and a fanatical criminal operation have originated? What made the scenario likely, if anything?

The constable had told him of the family's heir being often abroad and not involved in the railway business much at all: never at ceremonies, missing board meetings, etc. The constable's boss, the superintendent himself, was sometimes asked to these meetings and had never seen him there. When he did appear in Aberdeen, it was apparently to go to large social functions arranged by the parents, probably in hopes of seeing him settle down, for the constable had intimated that the Old Man did not seem so proud of his son as such a man ought to be. He spent his time at home with his daughter and wife and didn't bother going abroad with his son. Heaven knew what the young man was doing on his own on the Continent, the constable had said under his breath.

Barton decided to approach the fishermen, cautiously, to probe them on the family, the plans, and all the baseless gossip that could be had.

* * *

"Good e'en," said Barton gruffly but courteously, trying to gauge the attitude of the fishermen as he approached.

"E'en," replied a couple that glanced his way before returning to their low-voiced talk.

Barton was still in his vagrant disguise and chose his angle accordingly.

"You men know if that house there be lived in?"

" 'Tisn't," replied one.

This was going to be harder than he thought.

"Anyone coom to check it, like?"

"Nay, not anymoor," said another.

"Anymoor?" Barton echoed, picking up on both the accent and the implication. "Doosn't look to've been used recently, t'be sure."

"Not by reg'lar folk," said the man. "Not for a home, no."

After a pause, Barton asked, "What for, then?"

"We dinna know," said another man, "but it was only in the dark, and a lamp would be burning."

Barton considered. He began to wonder if the house had been used to train Agnes and probably others using hypnosis. He would need to investigate this further after this so-called conversation was over; for now, he needed to get more gossip out of these laconic fellows.

Without being asked, however, one of the nearer men looked at him curiously, his hands not stopping in their net-mending task, and said, "D'ye know yer the second man to be askin' sich questions in as many nights? That's mighty queer, I would say, eh?" he nodded to another chap farther from the center of their rough circle.

"Aye. A'would," the other returned, fixing Barton with a stare that made his stomach turn over.

As the question of why he wanted to know translated itself from the fierce man's eyes to his mouth, Barton calculated his options. He could try to continue with his beggar act but then he wouldn't be able to ask about other salient details. The alternative was shifting into his detective persona but he wasn't sure if these nocturnal inhabitants of such a starched-up town would feel comforted by the law, or baited by it, calm as they looked at the moment. And who had been asking questions the night before? Barton thought.

Barton decided to drop the act. He focused his gaze on the asker. "I've come to find a woman. I fear she's in a desperate situation—in much danger." He had the attention of the whole group now, which sat stock-still and felt the electricity behind his words, coming as they did from his heart.

"It has to do with this town and a certain family—" he checked himself. "A number of certain families," he continued, feeling a sudden rage against the rich, both those he had been working with and the one he'd been foiled by at the inn. They weren't the ones hurt, were they?

"And an old man who goes by the name Tunbridge. He performs some sort of hypnotism to put people under his control." There was a barely-heard wave of perception as breaths were taken and seats shifted.

A charged silence settled on the scene, which Barton knew from long negotiations with witnesses not to break. He felt the pull between different men in front of him but did not look directly at them, waiting with his head down.

Finally he felt a hand on his shoulder. "We've no' got a Tunbridge. One here's a Zelazny," he said, as another man spat.

"We thought they might be getting the place ready to be redone, working there nights, but why so quietly? Jed here did a walk 'round one night and saw who 'twas."

"Was a bunch of queer-looking young folk, all sitting on the floor, not sayin' a word," said the man Jed. "And in the back where the lamp was, the old man talked to one of 'em at a time—for hours. Always at night while fishing boats were goin' out, when a passenger ship had come in that morning. Verra suspicious-like. So we been watching," he finished.

"Haven't seen any lights in there for months, since well before the plans were cancelled," said the fierce man. "You think they're related?" he asked, obviously aware that Barton knew more than he had yet let on.

"Aye," Barton sighed. The older man who had spat at the name Zelazny claimed his attention.

"One of those young folk was my son. Taken at fourteen, he was. No word where he's gone. Know it was them as took 'im. Known it for a year now—the bastards—but they vanished into thin air."

Barton let a pause descend before asking, "Has it started up again?"

A beat, then Jed raised his eyes to Barton's. "Last night, just after t'other fellow left, name o'

Henderson—said he were a reporter. Doot that."

"All right," said Barton, looking around the now-attentive circle. He knew not to embarrass them by thanking them aloud. "Now what about the boats? A passenger ferry comes every morning? And when do fishing boats go out and come back?" he asked.

"Come in every morning 'cept Sunday," replied Jed. "And another one sets out just before. Bound for Hull," he said, before Barton could say the question aloud.

"Fishing boats leave 'tween t'ree and five in the mornin', come back around dinner time, high noon."

Barton nodded, trying out scenarios in his mind. If the villains had been here since their departure from the inn—no, that wasn't reasonable, since the light had only started last night. They may have stopped somewhere else on their journey and only arrived yesterday. Were they still here or had they departed by the ferry? And who were they? Was it the same man with the chloroform, another henchman of the Chatsworths, or someone from the Russian crime gang? His head was swimming in possibilities as he tried to form the most likely timeline.

"No lamp tonight, then?" he said finally.

The closest man shook his head no.

"All right. I've got one last question. What

do you know of young Chatsworth?"

Another wave traveled through the group, this one more violent.

"I know he left this mornin' on the ferry for Hull—is it 'im? Mixed up in the kidnappin' and all?" said the man who had spat, a suppressed rage making his voice tremble.

"He left this… did he have company?"

Glances were exchanged, faces interrogated without words.

"Aye," said the fierce man. "A young woman."

Chapter 52

Barton slept in the back of the quay shed, to be called if the fishermen saw any lights. He thought over what he'd heard, trying to separate the possible from the likely, resorting to sounding his instincts about the different criminals he'd encountered. Tunbridge, from the MacFarlanes' reports, was bold elsewhere in the country; would he be covert here? Was there another man in his position that directed operations from here in Aberdeen, using the old public building? How much did the Chatsworths know, both the father and the son?

It appeared that the son was involved. He would wait to hear about the father from the Mac-Farlanes after their call on him the next morning. He also needed to return to the police office to check the early morning post in case there was news of this Tunbridge character at work elsewhere.

He weighed all this as the midnight hours ticked into early morning, not getting much rest.

No lamp had shone in the house across the road. The fishermen, who had taken him for a righteous sort of man, had not woken him until the sun was mostly risen, near seven o'clock.

He immediately pulled on his coat, thanked the gruff messenger for the call, and asked whether anything further had occurred out of the ordinary.

A smile curled the edge of his lip. "Jis' you," he said.

Barton gave him a look, acknowledging, but not encouraging, the grim humor. He was in no mood for gallows humor today; he had dreamt terrible things in the past half-hour and his heart was still racing.

"I'll be going to check for some messages. I should return by mid-morning," he said, with a glance at the empty quay. "Have the others gone?"

"Aye, we leave to go home when the boats go out; that's our night's rest. We come back after dinner, which is our breakfast, ye might say," said the messenger. "I've stayed fer ye."

Barton realized it was the man whose son had been taken. He grasped his shoulder; they nodded to one another. The older man left first, then after a pause Barton left to head in the opposite direction, toward the center of town.

Chapter 53

As the detective knocked on the side door to the police station, he realized there would be no message from London if Sergeant Ragby had been able to interfere with operations. The timeline made it a possibility but still he hoped someone might have sent him some information about the hypnotist.

Messages had arrived. Those of his friends who had gone into law in London replied quickly. One had heard of a Tunbridge; one had not. The one who had heard of him believed him to have done some mischief at some northern university and been run out of town on a rail, nothing more. The one who had not heard the name Tunbridge, however, given the profile, related a story of harrowing similarity.

The letter read:

I saw a trial in the city several years ago where two witnesses were called to speak for a man up for treason. It caused quite a stir; you must have heard about it, Gerry, even in your backwater. The man being tried had been apprehended mainly by accident, as he attempted to send a bomb through the post. It had been addressed to the Duke of Beaufort.

The witnesses called on his behalf were of foreign extraction and from the same region as the man, somewhere in the northern reaches of the Russian empire, if I recall correctly. And the way they acted was even more memorable than the charge leveled. Both the man and the woman were ushered into the court with their heads down. They only made eye contact when directed to by the head bailiff and answered questions in a most peculiar low monotone. They appeared compliant and gave ready answers, all of which corroborated the defendant's barely believable alibi.

When they were dismissed, they left in the same manner: head down, a trance-like shuffle, almost as if they were sleep-walking. Several months after the trial had concluded, it was reported in the Observer that this same witness—the man —had been found in the Thames, all identification gone. Luckily, the dredging up of the body was overseen by an inspector who'd been at the trial and been most impressed by the gentleman's queer comportment. He recognized him even after drowning.

The lady was never seen or heard from again, as she had left the house where she had been staying during the trial with no word of where she was bound.

I was momentarily saddened upon thinking of it because it was a beautiful woman—and I believe now she and the man must have been somehow hypnotized to bear false witness, long before any of the officers of the court knew such tools of treachery were available. The traitor had been released—an older man, short, bristly white hair and beard, thinnish lips and a broad forehead—because of insufficient counter-evidence. He was also not heard from again. His name was—I looked it up—Turnowsky.

Barton re-read the letter to memorize all the details his friend had related, grateful for his perspicacity. It joined the pile to be burnt.

At Grantham, his letters fell into the hands of men he did not know but they replied faithfully, "No further news to report on your hypnotist character."

In York, his early associates were now men of business and industry; they returned rumors that he could ask the MacFarlanes to confirm: the competition for rail monopoly and customers was fierce enough that underhanded dealings were not unknown to happen in order to lay new track and sign new freight. Another rumor attached a series of kidnappings to the Selby-MacFarlane line through Glasgow.

Other details from those sources included a description of the fierce Chatsworth-MacFarlane rivalry, the uncertainty with which the community regarded the younger MacFarlanes' takeover of their father's business empire, and the whispers of some scandal touching the MacFarlanes that had been kept under wraps. The last one Barton could have told the sender a little more about.

All this had been written in letters sent to Leeds, care of the police office, which had been redirected to Aberdeen, at his earlier direction. He wondered now whether the information helped at all when combined with what he'd learned about the old public rooms of the Chatsworths'. Which leads to follow? Did they all hang together? He withdrew and headed toward the hotel where his allies were waiting.

"Oh, Detective! One moment. This just came for you as well," said the constable. He handed him a folded telegram that he'd just gotten from the machine in the hallway of the station. Barton read:

TUNBRIDGE IS TURNOWSKY IS BERZINSH BUT NOT ZELAZNY STOP HAS JUST DISCOVERED ACT OF C AND LEFT

COUNTRY STOP
-E

There was no originating address, just the "E" of the signature but Barton had no difficulty guessing who'd been able to link the aliases of their hypnotist and send him the information: that Ellers whom the MacFarlanes raved about, particularly Horace, as a Crown agent secretly on their side. Well, and where is he now? Barton thought. If our link with the Russian hypnotizing organization has left the country, it only remains to get the "C" whose act brought all of us Carknocke County people into the plot.

Chapter 54

Henry MacFarlane had already risen and been mildly alarmed at their one ally's non-appearance by seven o'clock. He went down to breakfast in the dining room. Horace still slept.

As he sat in the dining room on the first floor, Henry could see the street below. He sipped his tea and read his paper but all the while his eyes darted to the action in the street below. Finally his eyes alighted on what he was seeking: the detective, in plain clothes, was walking by slowly, across the street. Henry recognized him by his dusty clothes and cap of disguise from yesterday. He was puzzled why he had not changed and did not enter the hotel. He looked around for other signs but could not see the entrance itself, as it was directly underneath his window.

As he watched, the person he thought to be the detective strolled off to the west. What was going on? MacFarlane thought to himself. Had that in fact been Barton or were his eyes playing tricks on him? What was he up to?

As he evaluated the options and finished his cold toast, Henry decided that Barton must be following his own trail; he would simply have to trust him.

Horace made his entrance to the dining room, a bit disheveled-looking but determined. They spoke in low tones about how to handle the interview with Old Man Chatsworth that morning.

* * *

In a nearby pub, Barton considered whether it was necessary to make contact with the brothers yet. Should he send them word that he was continuing his search or would they soldier on without him and trust him to meet with them later? He had not liked the look of the person standing on the street near the hotel entrance, eyeing all who entered, and occasionally consulting something in his pocket that looked like a photograph. Highly suspicious—if only the concierge had noticed.

He decided to send a cryptic note: "Following fish to find bait. Rooms watched. Meet after dinner at her saint's church." He sent it with a boy hanging around the pub door, instructing him to give it only to a Henry or Horace MacFarlane at the Albert Hotel.

Now he was free to follow the trail. He'd slept—a little—eaten—a little—and could now wait for the Chatsworth news. His messages made him believe that the fishermen were his best lead even if unverified. Perhaps a visit to the ticket office for that ferry…

He found it unattended. After quickly studying the scheduled ferry ports—there were fewer than a dozen—he stepped behind the counter to find the record from the day before. It listed only one ship, the Maitland, which had sailed for Hull at 8 o'clock in the morning. Today's ship, a smaller one called Red's Bounty, had sailed this morning, also at eight o'clock, just after he had left the docks.

No one was coming, it seemed. Perhaps the ferry master's schedule was dictated as the dockhands' was and the man was now home asleep. Barton did not like to count on such a 'perhaps.' He lifted the book of manifests from underneath the port records and scanned the passengers' names for any he might recognize.

Out of the fifty or so passengers, most had been lower class tickets: people who would stand on the deck for the few hours' journey south through the North Sea. Among those who had purchased first-class tickets, which allowed for a sitting lounge and a tea service, he saw no Chatsworths, which he had anticipated. No Tunbridges either. A good number of Dutch-looking names, as was to be expected from Hull's continental routes. Of the English ones, he could see none he might relate to earlier clues or known aliases.

"Blast," he said, under his breath.

* * *

It was nearing noon by the time Barton had finished at the ferry office and then searched the perimeter of the empty town building for any clues. He'd gone in a wide circle from the road to the shore and back behind the house. There was a bracken field leading up to a twenty-foot cliff at the water's edge. He quartered the wooded area between the house and the town but found no evidence of who might be coming or going or why. He decided to stick with his theory of someone running a squad of hypnotized individuals for the Russian crime gang and this person somehow being related to the Chatsworths.

This thought almost made him laugh with the absurd sound of it but then Barton thought of how to undo the hypnotism. He stopped up short in his slow walk to try to remember if he had heard at any point what the remedy was, for if he did encounter any of those 'queer-looking young folk' in that house, he would want to release them from their mental prison—but how?

He had never attended one of the assemblies, Agnes had not known about them herself, and Horace had not related his experience in Berwick-Upon-Tweed in detail. His contacts' letters, while helpful on hypnotized behavior, did not explain how to exit the state. He started to feel a knot of panic in his chest but battled it down, considering his options.

He would investigate the house now, which would likely be empty, then return to speak to the MacFarlanes at the hotel, provided the eye at the door was gone. If there was something, or someone, in the house, he could hang back and call on the MacFarlanes or the fishermen for aid. Expelling a breath and his panic, Barton strode from his place among the trees to the back entrance of the house.

He opened the back door with his most common lock-pick and found himself in a kitchen. All Barton's senses were on alert. He smelled the dust and some alcoholic cleaning agent. He noticed the dead silence that meant all the windows were closed and no ventilation was flowing through. He passed through the hall to the sitting rooms, the long ballroom, and the dining room, all decorated in a fancy style from forty years past.

There was no furniture in the rooms except a few items under cloths and pushed into corners. Barton investigated these in the ballroom first, careful to disturb as little of the layers of dust as possible. Nothing. In the dining room, nothing but old, warped chairs.

The stairway was located in the middle of the house, running straight up to a landing on the back wall, then crossing back toward the front. His steps made the stairs creak and he felt exposed but he reached the top without incident. His ears picked up a sound in the still-dead silence: a slow, rasping sound—or two sounds, rather—in concert. He looked down from the second-story window and saw no one in the field leading to the water but a figure was walking along the roadside a little ways off. Barton didn't recognize the man but he realized he might be coming to the house; he backed away quickly to search the upstairs rooms.

One side held a walking room with alcoves and a balcony on the front: no furniture. Thick layers of dust. Curtains smelling of sea salt and mildew. He crossed the hall and stopped outside the door to the other side, listening. He could hear the rasping here more clearly. Was it two breaths?

He took a deep breath through the nose himself and turned sharply at what he smelled: two recently lit tallow candles stood in sconces at either side of the door. Their pungent smell indicated they had not lain dormant for as long as the furniture in the other rooms. Excitement rising again, Barton turned the door handle to find it locked.

He knelt to look through the keyhole but could see nothing but a large marble fireplace and mantel. He was becoming more worried by the minute about the man coming down the lane and the sounds on the other side of the door but could hardly think which was the rational course of action at this point.

If it were Agnes behind that door, he would batter it down. He pushed down the swell of feeling he had while thinking this, forcing himself to think through the possible consequences. He thought of his lock picks again but risked a look through the window again before proceeding. The man had stopped at the gate to the lane and seemed to be smoking a pipe. What the devil? He rushed back to the door, pulled out his picks, and hoped for some luck.

The third one toggled the lock just right and pushed the bolt back. He opened the door slowly, entering with his view toward the front window. It was another walking room with a large bay window to the front. He peered around toward the back and his heart had reason to falter.

Past the fireplace, which was not in use, there was a large straw mattress, badly covered in graying white sheets, holding three sleeping figures under another gray-white sheet, which was pulled up to their chins and tucked in tightly to prevent movement.

Barton advanced slowly. There were three women, and the far one was Agnes. She was the source of one of the rasping sounds, as she looked pale and sick again, not lively and spirited as she had been after her many weeks in the countryside.

The woman next to her was in worse condition, a healing blackened eye giving a greenish-yellow tinge to an otherwise handsome face. The third woman, nearest the fireplace, was more homely—her thin, light hair framed a pale face—but at least her breathing was quiet and he didn't see any injuries.

Barton stepped to Agnes, his emotions veering wildly from elation at having found her to a blind rage at finding her thus and a mute helplessness as to how he could help any of these women. He tugged at the sheet, pulling it down from neck-level to waist-level, glad that at least they all wore shifts.

There was an immediate response from all three: their breathing became more normal and they opened their eyes but continued gazing at the ceiling.

Barton gently touched Agnes' shoulder, calling her name at a low pitch. No response. He tried again, then used her original name: 'Euphemia.'

She turned her face slightly and her eyes locked with his without recognition. Now his thoughts whirled toward despair, since this is what he was not prepared for: how to end this curse of hypnotism. He choked back a sob of frustration and once again forced himself to consider all the pieces in play—the man outside.

Barton eased closer to the front to see what

the man was doing now: tapping his pipe against his leg and swinging open the gate to walk down the lane. Barton formed his plan and hurried to pull the sheet back over them, which closed all the women's eyes instantly. A shiver went up his spine as he stepped away to lock the door and conceal himself in the opposite room.

Chapter 55

After a few moments, Barton heard the clumping up the stairs of a heavy tread, which creaked the old wood worse than his own feet had. The smell of the pipe reached him next. He couldn't see him but felt the man's unhurried pace and heard the keys jostle from his pocket before the door creaked open again. Barton allowed himself a sigh of relief. Now if only his visit could continue to go undetected...

The dead air of the place was not much broken by the noises the visitor made; it seemed to envelop them as he moved and spoke—for speak he did—in a low, tender mumble. Barton moved from the opposite wall to the door-jamb to hear better.

"S'only ol' Patrick so's ye don't disturb, aye. Time for a sup' fer all o' ye, and up!" And he whipped away the sheet with a flourish, its nap crackling.

He continued, "S'only old Patrick, 'tis true,

but a's the one as keeps ye alive, no? Keeps o' secrets, noon the wiser, aye."

Barton heard a bottle stopper being pulled out with a pop, the glug-glug of liquid being poured. So this was their jailer. He wondered who was paying him to 'keep o' secrets.' He was glad at least that it was not the hypnotizer–in-chief, whom he assumed would be more circumspect in securing the house.

His thoughts again churned through the information filed in his head, trying to remember if anyone had indicated the trigger to stop the trance but his attention was caught by the new noises coming from the room: the man's ragged breathing and fast, coaxing words.

"Tha's right, Bessie, my girl, easy-like. You'll like it," followed by a grunt from him. "I promise, there, love," he said.

Barton could hear the straw mattress crackling as he imagined the man climbing atop one of the young women. No, I shall not allow that! He crossed the hallway, checking the window for others approaching: none. He stepped into the room and, grabbing the tossed-away sheet, leapt wildly to circle the man's neck with it.

The man Patrick had not noticed Barton's entrance as he spoke to himself and the girl. Barton caught him as he was kneeling on the bed near the third figure, closest to the fireplace, patting her cheek with one hand while the other reached down for her shift. Barton guessed how the middle woman had gotten her bruise and black eye and a rage flowed through his limbs as he squeezed the sheet round the man's throat. The bulky form thrashed and grabbed, throwing his weight to the side to try to disturb Barton's balance but he was firm, focused on maintaining his grip and squeezing the life from the stout blackguard.

After a minute, the strength behind the motions was drained from his limbs and he dropped like a stone in Barton's arms. Barton laid him down carefully, still holding the sheet ready in case he was faking. But no, his face was purple, his mouth was open—had he killed him? Before checking, he tied the man's hands and feet together. He stepped back; he looked dead.

He thought of his sister Jenny's husband, who he'd wanted to murder every time he saw her confined to her bed due to 'a fall,' or 'a tumble.' Now he'd actually killed a man. Even though it had been necessary, he felt guilty. And what would the Board of Police say, even if they managed to solve this case? He stopped the fearful thoughts, left the man on the floor, and crossed to the straw bed.

The pale young blonde woman lay with her dress bunched up around her waist, her hands at her sides, her eyes still staring upward. Barton choked back another sob of desperate frustration and pulled the white cloth down. Still not out of the trance! What was he to do now?

He tried calling names, waving his hands in front of their eyes, squeezing their hands. After several minutes of hand-wringing, he realized he was acting hysterical and made an effort to slow his breathing, sitting down to close his eyes. The back-draft of the rage he had felt now plunged him into a black state where he had trouble thinking. His mind was in denial of the insistent visual imagery; he couldn't blot out the image of the poor homely girl, completely unresponsive, with that oaf on top of her. He abandoned thinking and tried to steady his shaky breathing, slowing its pace after a few minutes.

He said Euphemia's name again; she turned.

"What is her name?" he asked, pointing to the pale blonde.

"Diana," she answered. His pulse picked up again.

"How do I wake her up?" he asked, hope kindling.

She stared at him, not seeing him. Damn.

Chapter 56

While Barton was still sizing up the house
and its inhabitants, the MacFarlanes had been allowed entry through the massive gates of the property of Thomas Chatsworth, Esq. The reluctance of
the day before was gone or at least masked better
with civility. They were shown into a large library
where shelves of books lined one wall and windows twice the height of a man marched along
another. They were seated at a long conference
table of rich black walnut. It was not so much a
difference of quality they noted, as they compared
it to their own business headquarters in Leeds and
Glasgow and London, but the pervasive feeling that
everything was persistently older, the dust and
mildew displayed almost proudly.

Thomas Chatsworth himself appeared, looking the same as he had the previous times when
either of the MacFarlanes had seen him: a sturdy
gentleman of about sixty years, medium height, a
white beard and wispy grey hair remaining. His

dark eyes, soft with age, regarded them now, doing their best to appear piercing yet persuasive.

"Good morning, gentlemen. It has been a very long while since I have had the pleasure of a competitor's company, now that Robert keeps most things in hand, but welcome. What can I do for you?"

He asked this question in a tone that suggested he would do nothing. But Horace had anticipated this attitude and they had concocted a strategy. Horace gave Henry the barest glance before nodding assertively to Chatsworth.

"I do not attempt to deny that we are hard at work competing with you and doing it well. We are not here in dire straits, as you might have thought, to beg to be bought." Horace paused; he'd marked the old man's blink and his head jerking slightly backward, as if he'd heard a loud noise.

He continued. "No, we are here because we know you are running a side business which flouts common decency and betrays the Empire which we are all working to protect and expand. Whether you know it or not," he added, as Chatsworth's face showed no hint of knowledge or defensiveness.

Chatsworth spluttered a denial but Henry cut him off.

"It must therefore be your son, sir, who has 'most things in hand,' as you said. He is aligned with a treacherous, anarchic political organization which is tasked with nothing less than sowing mayhem and chaos in powerful countries such as ours."

"This is an absolutely ridiculous accusation; I will not tolerate it," Chatsworth said, his features flushing red. "You cannot have any proof that this is so and therefore I call it the most infamous slander. You have not had the gall to mention this accusation to anyone else yet, have you?" Not waiting for an answer, he rushed on, "Because it must stop here. I'll have you in jail for suggesting any such thing, gentlemen as you are not—"

Horace withdrew from his letter-case a sheaf of papers showing many columns of numbers. The old man stopped shouting to stand and grab them, reading closely without any glasses to hand.

"This is just a bunch of passenger manifests! What do you mean by presenting this?"

Horace produced another sheaf, thicker this time, with names as well as numbers.

"This is the accompanying information which certifies that many poor, young, ignorant, and solitary travelers entered Scotland on your trains and never exited, according to public record."

"Where did you get that? This is a preposterous conclusion. You have no proof a judge would deem worthy of the name. Perhaps they got lost?"

Horace presented a third folder, removing a sheet of paper with a list of places this time. His research about the railway crimes in the past six months had actually come in handy, though not as originally thought.

"And these are the places where there have been monstrous experiments on these young people, using hypnotism to override their will and compel them to commit hideous acts."

Henry finally saw a bit of a shock reflected in the man's face as he scanned through the list and recognized his company's station-stops. It made his movements jerky; he thrust the page back to Horace before falling back into his chair.

They waited through the tense silence, trying to sense where the man, so violently confronted with his son's possible misdeeds, would fall, whether into denial or capitulation. They hoped for the latter but were prepared for the more likely route.

"If it's not you, it's your son, sir. We need to know where he is, in order to stop his plans," said Horace, taking the aggressive interviewer role.

"You—but how do you connect my son with all those people, and places, and misdeeds? It seems an awfully illogical leap to make, especially as there is no evidence you've shown that—" here he stood again, pointing a meaty fist. "You're just trying to cow me into confessing to something! I've never been subjected to such a scheme in my whole life—this is unheard of and will not be borne

—"

Horace took the photograph of Agnes from his pocket and held it at Chatsworth's eye level. Recognition finally dawned and he sank back down. Horace exchanged a glance with Henry; this had been a gamble. He had intended to wring information out of him with Agnes' sad tale, but perhaps he knew more of it already than they did.

"She's gone, isn't she? Is that what you're about to tell me? She was one of the missing?" he said in a strange, defeated voice.

"She was found but kidnapped again. We believe she may be here, under your—"

"Robert introduced her as a young lady at a party we had—as a joke. I fiercely disapproved but he said it was some necessary sort of test. This was last year. She was—she was ever so gentle and quiet, I did not see what he was doing but play-acting and parading his indecorous self—but what, what has he been doing?"

Here he raised his aged brown eyes, now much confused, to Horace, and hoped in vain for something less than he expected.

So they had not retrieved any useful new information from Thomas Chatsworth, Esq. However, they had convinced him of their theory, which went a good way to proving it to themselves. Now for finding the man managing the escapade.

Chapter 57

Weighing all their options, which were few, the brothers decided to return to the hotel to regroup. They also hoped that the detective would find a way to reunite with them there. They received his note from a dirty boy running after them as they left the lobby for their rooms and were relieved to at least have news of his intent.

They'd been in the room a couple of hours going through theories and had just called for a late lunch when Horace looked out the window and spied the same man who had been hanging around the entrance at their return. He was now across the street and visible from their room, easy to spot in his orange and blue vest.

Horace said, "I believe that is the 'friend' Barton warned us about. Still there."

Henry came to look and said, "Well, let's hope he finds a way around him this time since we have at least some good ground gained to relate to him. But where to move next…"

"Chatsworth said his son had been off to France; do we follow? Or is it a ruse? And if so, by father or by son?" said Horace, reiterating a previous pathway of thought. "I rather believe the old man at this point but that doesn't help us get any closer to the truth."

"I agree. I think young Robert must have been lying about an awful lot—extra working hours, meetings in far countries, absence at family events or at the breakfast table. I imagine a double life can be very exhausting. The son's explanation that things were busy and that our firm was mainly to blame may have been enough for the father. Who knows? Maybe men are less likely to see the light when it involves their sons, as well."

"Or fathers," Horace said, giving his brother a rueful grimace.

Henry sighed, stretching his limbs and shaking his head.

"Quite. Now we suppose that Robert Chatsworth is somehow working with the Zemlya i volya and that he is recruiting their—let's say raw materials. They are training them psychologically, and perhaps physically, to perform certain feats in order to cause trouble for the stable monarchies that remain in Europe."

"With you so far but what does he gain from it? Maybe the younger Chatsworth did actually cause this side-adventure in order to dishonor us and gain market share and that is why he entered into such a devil's agreement. But was his lashing out at us condoned or did he act on his own? And if the latter, wouldn't the higher-ups in charge be angry at that? So far, we haven't seen signs of any retribution."

"No, but keep in mind they may be working units independent of one another. Everything does not necessarily feed up a chain of command."

"All right. If the masterminds don't know and never find out, what would be the organization's next move if Agnes is recovered? Is that who we want to follow? Or leave that to than man Ellers and keep to the industrial competitor that got us involved in the first place?" Horace said, exasperated.

"I think that depends on whether we are fully out of danger, for one, and what Barton will now do with this information, for two. He may have struck out on his own against his sergeant—"

"We can all tell why he did that," Horace said.

Henry let the interjection hang in the air until it felt snide. He said softly, "I don't know that we can, Horace, but if he loves her, what can be wrong in that?"

"Nothing's wrong with it, of course, it's just so damn inappropriate—and simple bad timing!"

Another pause while the door was opened

and lunch was delivered.

An uneasy silence ensued while Henry sliced his ham and mustard and Horace deboned his roast chicken.

Horace felt the need to break it first. "All right, I'll leave it alone. What do we think he'll do? And what has he been doing here, anyway, for two days?"

Henry cleared his throat, taking a swallow of the Albert Hotel's good claret, before responding. "We will have to wait. I'm sure he'll have an explanation at the church when we meet him this evening. He's an honest type, Horace, you can't deny him that."

"Of course not—that's what makes him so bloody hard for me to understand!" he exclaimed with a half-laugh aimed at lightening his mood of frustration.

It worked; they finished lunch in better humor.

Chapter 58

The bones and the dishes were still on the small table when the door opened silently hours later, producing a man in torn, stained clothing. The brothers were dozing in their chairs, tired of waiting and being cooped up. The man stepped to Henry and touched his arm. His eyes sprang open.

Barton put a finger to his lips to indicate silence and beckoned Henry to the window. There was the orange and blue vest still, talking to another man—this one small and wiry and dressed in baggy, shapeless clothes. As they watched, he loped off in a queer run. The other man flashed a glance in their direction but they were hiding at the sides of the casement.

Barton then took Henry outside the door to their rooms where a narrow panel in the wall stood open. Henry poked his head into the panel and saw a passage to the exterior wall and stairs leading both down and up. Barton closed the panel and studied its outline, then checked all the other hallway panels near their rooms. One other gave him pause; he pressed his ear to the wood.

Something made him jerk his head back. Henry continued to watch, not sure what was happening. Barton pulled out a long piece of flat metal from his jacket, carefully placed it to the side of the panel then drove it in and jerked it down in two swift, forceful motions.

The outline of the panel didn't budge, but the part where Barton had his makeshift crowbar splintered. Henry saw him thrust the back end of the bar upward into the hole.

They heard a large grunt and the sound of something falling. Barton then spoke, "Quick, help me pull the rest open," and as their hands pulled the panel outward, Henry saw another small, wiry figure inside the corridor. He was slumped into a sideways heap with a head wound that was starting to bleed. Barton grabbed the body, pulled it out from the wall, and dragged it into their rooms. Henry tried to close the panel and make it look as unobtrusively damaged as possible, sweeping up the large splinters and tossing them into the fireplace.

"Now," he said, as they closed the door to their rooms, and Horace was making awake noises, "may we hear what that was all about?"

Barton dropped the corridor man near the fireplace and said, "First we'll tie this one up to restrain him when he wakes."

They did this with drapery rope from the back wall of curtains, Horace projecting an unhappily mystified air.

"You may have—" started Barton, but then changed tack. "They have heard. You. Have you been discussing anything of importance?" Their alarmed glance informed him.

"Yes, well, nothing we can do about it now. When I arrived, I knew to dodge the same annoying man who's been there since we arrived—do you know yet who he works for? No? Right—but then I noticed that a man coming out the back alley went up to talk to him directly, so I followed his path. It leads to an unused—as far as I can tell—servants' stair. I came out the one side but I figured they might have merely changed shifts. I checked the other, on the other side of your door and, hearing a slight noise, was able to dispatch the eavesdropper.

"But there is much more to say and much more to be done, which I fear we should discuss now instead of later when we will have another spy trading shifts, even though I am so very, very tired," he finished, and plopped himself into an armchair.

After the brothers recovered from their shock, they asked what to do with the eavesdropper. They were also a little in awe of the detective, whom they had so recently been discussing as a faint-hearted romantic and who was now wielding weapons with skill and not batting an eyelash at concealing a captive in a gentleman's rooms.

"All right, then. Start with your discoveries and we'll finish with ours, which won't take long," said Henry.

Barton told them everything he thought could be of importance, from the enlightening gossip of the fishermen, to his reconnaissance of the house, to finding its 'inhabitants,' to witnessing the man's approach. He let the implication of some wrongdoing hang in the air as motivation for his killing of the man but did not go into detail.

He ended with his attempts to waken each of the women from their state without success.

Horace interrupted him. "But I have witnessed one of these so-called séances and they use a voice command! It's one word that wakes them but it may be different... the one I heard, what was it..." he murmured.

Henry spoke as well. "When I talked to the rector, he said it was clapping three times that did it. That might work for the others. We can try both," he said, looking at Horace. He was still trying to remember his word but nodded back.

Henry spoke again. "And about this Robert Chatsworth, we may be closer to ground on that one."

"That is well, as all I was able to gather is that he is out for this day and will likely return tomorrow—probably without the girl, whom he'll have sold off somewhere," Barton said.

"Yes," said Henry. "We had a little more background from Mr. Chatsworth about that. Robert is doing most of the travel and operations management for their business interests. He is often on the Continent and spends quite a bit of money, which his father thinks is on lavish parties and social outings. You know, generosity," he said.

"He has also been introducing here, into his own household, ladies of a certain disposition as acquaintances, which his father feels are beneath him and highly unsavory affairs. People of their circle—their trusted neighbors—engage them in conversation and Robert has what he calls his 'test.' I deduce that it is a test for their hypnotized victims to function without their controller and complete their missions. Do you agree?"

Horace stared. He said, "It is such a dreadful business. Why do it at all?"

"Profit is one answer," Barton responded. "Despicable cruelty to other human beings is another. And political radicalism is a third. Take your pick."

"I do doubt whether the political question enters into Chatsworth's calculations," said Henry.

"They could be using this organization entirely as a tool for their own ends. We can't know, at this point."

There was a pause. Barton eyed the MacFarlanes, "Will you come back with me then, to the house? We can remove the women from that situation and perhaps watch for Robert's return in the morning."

"Yes, I think that's the necessary next step," said Henry.

Horace still looked absent, deep in thought, until all of a sudden he burst out, "Zornhau!"

Chapter 59

They left the hotel separately in the early evening light, using both of the now-unoccupied secret corridors and leaving behind their still-sleeping captive. The three men approached the coastline of Aberdeen and Horace whistled at the sight. It was a picturesque scene but they did not linger to enjoy it, hurrying down together toward the dock end.

The fishermen with their nets and baskets had returned and looked with a measuring eye toward them. Jed noticed their coming and stepped out to meet Barton. He led them to the shack shelter before clasping his hand and nodding curtly at the other two. No introductions were expected.

"Has the young master returned by boat?" Barton asked.

"Nay, not he. Nor yet. But the Maitland returns tomorrow morning, 'a might be on tha' one."

"All right," said Barton. "Our thanks, Jed." And then turning to the brothers, "let's go."

They proceeded in single file across the field in silence.

Barton guided them into the house through the dusty rooms to the northern room upstairs. The man was still there: tied in twisted white sheets, he looked grey and very stiff. There was yet no smell but Barton dreaded the job to come: burying the lout outside in order not to attract animals or, he thought ironically, the police. Although he would bet no police had ventured near this place in years.

Henry was drawn to the straw pallet with its sleeping inmates. He observed the bruises of the middle one and their strained breathing. He seemed entranced himself as he asked, "What was the wake-up word you used, Barton?"

"I just said her name—her real name: Euphemia," and at this, her eyes opened again. Barton then said, "Diana," but she didn't stir. "There must have been different training systems, I conclude. Or maybe different passwords for each person to protect the larger mission, perhaps."

Now that she was awake, Henry clapped three times.

Three pairs of eyes watched hers as Agnes/Euphemia 'woke.' First her eyes tried to focus. Then her chin dropped to a natural angle and she began to truly look around, sitting up and noticing the three men, the room, the evening light,. When she glimpsed the man trussed and pushed to the side of the fireplace, she covered her mouth and said, "Oh!"

She gulped the air several times, fighting for self-mastery. She looked at them and Barton knew relief when her eyes found him and she said, "Tell me what has happened."

Henry looked pained and Horace preoccupied as Barton outlined the events since her kidnapping from the country inn, which she remembered.

"We don't know if you've been here the whole week you've been missing or whether there are other centres for these people but we are very lucky to have found you here in the first place we tried. Very lucky," he said quietly.

"We've been putting together evidence to try to find the motives behind—the purpose of your imprisonment. It looks to be related to a radical political movement." Then he asked, "Does that stir any memories?"

She shook her head, then stopped, her eyes glazing over. "Almost," she said. "So you were right, Mr. MacFarlane," she said to Horace. "Perhaps it will come to me. Go on."

"We think the Russian-Slavic movement called Zemlya I volya is somehow connected to Robert Chatsworth, the MacFarlanes' main competitor and it is he who has pulled us all into this plot, with his own hope of starting a scandal about the MacFarlanes. This scandal might be a sort of side-scheme to the main mission; the Zemlya group may not yet even know about it. They are the ringleaders who are organizing in secret, hypnotizing poor folk, and setting them to evil tasks."

Horace then spoke. "And in fact, we've put together several events and locations that link Chatsworth with a kidnapping and other crimes. We showed it to his father earlier today and he— well, he did not take it well."

"That's the main design, at any rate," Barton resumed. "And that is how we decided to search here for you. The fishermen of Aberdeen we have to thank for the information leading us here."

Agnes took a moment to consider what she'd heard and gave a small nod. "So, I was destined for something but was not successful, which is why I found myself used in some side-scheme, as you put it. They must have intended for me to stay here before being retrained or re-purposed somehow." She shuddered slightly and looked at her bedmates. "Can you wake them up as well? If we can, I think we should leave immediately," she said quietly.

Horace asked their names but awake, she no longer remembered them. Barton supplied the name she had said in trance and Horace repeated it in a louder tone than before, "Diana!"

The blond head turned and her eyes opened, unfocused, toward the ceiling.

"Now for my memory of the cure," Horace said. "Zornhau!" She exhibited the same refocusing motions as Agnes had, taking in the scene. The anxious lines forming showed the woman was already inching toward hysteria. Agnes put her hand on her arm and said, "Wait. We will have an explanation when she is also awake," and indicated the third young woman.

"Now what is her name?" Barton asked, and Agnes shrugged. Diana said, "Ellen. She 'as ma friend, befoor."

Agnes spun her head at this word. "You can remember before?"

"Aye, can ye no'?"

"No."

Horace once again boomed out, "Ellen," and the woman seemed to return to life more quickly than the other two. She sat up and turned toward Horace, her eyes not seeing but her other senses seeming keenly aware. Horace said, "Zornhau!" which made her laugh. She spoke, surprising everyone.

"Nay, nay, don't go in for that. I'm different from t'others, don't need no hip-nee-ism. They tell me I'm good at what I do, I dinna need it."

"And what do you do?" Barton asked, the first to recover his shock.

"I do errands for the gentlemen in places they dunno or dinna want to go. I ken the whole place, ye see, though I'm blind."

"Which place do you mean?" asked Horace.

"Why, Glasgow, o'cour', been 'ere all me life."

There was a pause as her audience absorbed the fact and tried to fit it with the rest of the puzzle.

"So," Agnes began, "you're from Glasgow, but do you know you're now in Aberdeen?"

"Nooo…" she returned. "They tol' me I'd be doing jobs fer 'em around t'east side where I'm from. They ne'er said anythin' aboot movin' oot tae 'nother city."

"And who are 'they?'" Horace asked.

"Why, the silly old German toffs who do the hip-nee-izing. Mister, what was it noow, Mister …" She twisted her head to think and rubbed her neck gently, at which the company enquired if she was hurt.

"Ay, 'tis a bit sore. D'ye see anytin'? I think his name was Zasny or something like. It'll coom to me," she continued.

"Yes," said Diana. "There's a very large bruise going blue and green."

"Is that Di?" Ellen said, smiling. "Then for sure we're in Glasgow and ye're mistaken. How did you coom in, Di? Are ye runnin' fer 'em too?"

The whole situation was in danger of becoming unhinged. Barton felt the need for order and stood. He said, "Let's stop and regain our bearings before we decide to do anything. Let's take a calm breath and think for a moment," he said, and paced away a few steps, regarding the man he'd strangled. Things had to become less unreal for him to think.

He turned back and tried to engage the gaze of each in the company. Diana looked mournful, blind Ellen looked strangely gay, Horace was regarding Ellen thoughtfully, Agnes was quiet and determined, and Henry looked to be fitting the pieces together.

"We think that one of the main men involved in this affair may be arriving by boat back to the harbor tomorrow morning. We all have the option therefore of leaving here now or waiting for his return to see where he goes, whether he is with anyone, and stopping him."

A frisson of disquiet visited those who listened.

Barton decided not to attempt to break through the defensive wall of imagination, or whatever it was, that the blind girl had fabricated. He would rely on the other four for direction and hope her friend could look after her. He still wasn't sure what Diana had meant by being a friend 'before,' but quizzing her could wait.

Horace glanced at the women to gauge their mood and said hesitantly, "I would prefer to stay and see if he returns, at least for tonight. I don't think there is danger in waiting here since the agent assigned to the place has been dispatched and there haven't been any others coming."

"That is a fair point. We will have to watch against any more that do come," said Barton.

"We can take turns," said Henry. "I'll take the first and wake one of you when I start to drift off—after a couple of hours."

Horace nodded. "I'll go next."

Agnes looked at them all. "This is a most strange and unpleasant situation we find ourselves in," she said, taking hold of Diana's hand. "And I who have come to know you since my—my being taken, trust in you and thank you for doing what is right." Here she gazed at Henry, then Barton, then Horace.

"I will explain what I understand to Diana and Ellen—" and she glanced at Ellen, who seemed to have grown in dignity and seriousness as she listened to the plan and Agnes' speech. "—So that they also may have some trust in you and think about their futures now as well. For when we leave, if it is tomorrow, we will have much to regain to become ourselves again."

Chapter 60

As night descended, the men withdrew toward the window, one to keep watch and the others to sleep, while the women stayed on the pallet and talked amongst themselves. As none of them would use the covers to warm themselves, the men left their coats, to provide them some modesty.

The night passed quietly, with the small conversation on the pallet subsiding in an hour, Diana rising to join Ellen on one side, who slept in her arms. Diana had managed to break it to her gently: whatever she had been told had been a lie. They had all likely been forced to do things they would not have done freely.

These two lay twined together and Agnes lay alongside, not truly sleeping but hugging the broad coat to her body and thinking things through, trying to find any useful information hiding in her mind. She was trying to picture, or remember, the 'main man' Barton had mentioned. Nothing came. Well, then, she really would have to trust her fine fellows, the three who had come to her rescue. Her distrust of the MacFarlanes, especially from her last encounter with Horace, had disappeared. She knew all three to be true: there was that crusade-like urgency in each man's gaze.

On the other side of the room, as Henry's turn to guard the walk passed uneventfully, he tried partly to listen to the murmured conversation, partly not to listen. He was also reviewing what he knew of Robert Chatsworth, how he might return, and what their best course of action would be when he did. Would he come here? Would he send someone here? That meant someone else to be killed or they would have to get out by the opposite way very quickly. If he came alone here, what then? They were an unlikely party to bind and interrogate a criminal.

No, that is when they should bring in the police—the higher order of police—to circumvent the circles they knew to be corrupted. But what to do in the moment… and what to do if he arrived by boat and never came near the house, keeping his hands lily-white? The thought burned in his mind; it would be the thought of all who kept watch that night as they mused through their silent turns.

* * *

They had all had a turn by two o'clock in the morning, and started their round again rather than wake the ladies. Finally it was past six o'clock and

Barton's final turn before they all stirred. He stared at the sea, trying to keep it in focus but periodically losing his gaze in the intensity of his thoughts. He regarded the room, and his eyes stopped again on the corpse near the fireplace. This might be the proper time to bury the man: under cover of dawn, before the fishing boats started coming in and more people were about. But tools, shovels?

He crept down the stairs quietly, seeing if there was aught to be used as a digging tool, while keeping an eye out the gap in the heavy drapery that showed him the front path.

There was a broken chair under one of the covers. He took two of the longer rods that made up the back: they might do. He laid them by the wall of the back room and went to wake the other men to help with the watching and digging but then he heard a sound.

It was very close and very quiet. Barton stopped moving to hear if it continued and heard it again: a muted tapping, which sounded like it was on wood, in the hallway. He crept into the hallway, glancing forward and seeing nothing through the dawn shadows. He edged back toward the door and wished there was a window alongside of it for him to peek out of but there was not. His heart lodged in his throat, a bird flapping in his lungs.

He drew his knife, picked up on the last trip to the hotel, and slid the bolt back and turned the knob ever so slowly, exposing the thinnest crack between the door and its jamb. A man was standing back from the door looking away toward the water.

At once, Barton's heart shrank back to its normal size as he recognized it was one of the fishermen who had gathered round him the night before last.

This man's salt-and-pepper hair was mostly covered with a close knit cap. He wore a rough-spun shirt and jacket over dark trousers stiffened with the salt sea air; he appeared in no hurry. Barton hissed softly and he turned then was motioned in. They stood just inside the door, Barton grasping the man's arm and clapping him on the shoulder, the other doing the same.

"What news?" said Barton.

"There is the boat sighted awa' off, coming into dock in an hour and a quarter. It be the one from the south where the young gentleman was gone," said the man. "And Jed bid me pass the news, that ye be ready in the case, as he saw ye were trying fer this place."

Barton nodded, squeezed his shoulder in gratitude. His downstairs errand came to his mind and he asked, "There is something I need to bury. How is the ground this morning: easy or hard?"

The man's expression jumped a bit as he asked but he replied, "Soft enough, we've no got the clay some others do, being in the river wash."

"Right. Good man. My thanks," said Barton, and the other went out the door, quickly disappearing in the fog.

That fog, thought Barton, a good thing and a bad. It will muffle our sounds of work but also hide from us anyone approaching. Best to work quickly, then. Before going upstairs, he glanced out the front window gap to make sure no one else approached.

He ascended and re-entered the room. The two women were still huddled together with Agnes behind them. She sat up slightly with a stillness and straightness that indicated she was not sleeping. He went to see—sure enough, her eyes were open. They found his. She mouthed, "News?" He nodded and cocked his head in the direction of the fireplace. She nodded slightly to show she had guessed what he needed to do next.

He went to wake the MacFarlanes and they thought about how to proceed. The man was utterly stiff with rigor mortis, which made carrying him easier, but they still needed two of them to do it. He returned to ask Agnes if she would watch from the top window and give them a bird-call signal if she saw anything. She nodded again, pulling the coat around her tightly and settling on the floor, leaning on the sill.

Barton and Henry took the limbs and Horace helped them down the staircase to avoid the sconces and the banister as they navigated back-wards.

They made it down, Horace scouting the path, and slipped out the door. Horace picked up the chair rods Barton indicated. They quickly elect-ed a spot downhill of the door, around the side of the building and away from the path. They could all feel time passing and the dawn lightening and therefore threw their backs into the digging work with their crude tools. They rotated the rest and after half an hour of sweaty work, as the sea air stuck close to them, had a hole large enough for a man but shallow enough for dogs to find.

"Since we cannot much hope to present this case in the light of day, I say this is the best course. We—I, at least, know him for a villain, and I have no qualms burying him here. Do you, gentlemen? We are deep in, now," said Barton.

"We are indeed deep in, man," replied Ho-race, wiping the sweat from his brow with his sleeve. "And I trust you in this as I have since I left Clatteringshaws."

As they tuned to Henry, he said, "I, too. There is no way we could have got this far without you. You have our trust and I'm sure I believe he's a villain. Nothing to stop me church-going, if that's what you are asking," he said with an attempt at humor.

"Ta," said Barton. "Then let's dig a little

deeper to make sure a rain or a dog doesn't unravel the whole deal." And they continued for another half hour as it got warmer and the wildlife started to make noises. They tossed the body in, finished filling the hole in much less time, scuffed around some of the topsoil plants they could find to hide the fresh look of the spot, and were ready to bound back up when they heard a low bird call, unrepeated and unjoined. Agnes.

They crept to the back door with as much speed and as little noise as they could, leaving the digging implements in a downstairs room and re-joining Agnes. She stood to the side of the front window, looking down on the path, and motioned for them to come quickly. The men did so and looked carefully down where she pointed.

A large, stocky man was coming on the road. He turned onto the path to their door. It was now light enough to see forms and shadows but the ocean mist blurred the edges of his clothes. He was followed by a smaller, more slender shadow. As the pair came closer, the second shadow showed bright blond hair under a fashionable bonnet.

Henry spoke to Agnes. "It doesn't look like the Robert I saw years ago, but do you know him?"

"From Diana's description, it is not Robert."

"Then what shall we do?"

"Detain them," said Barton. Agnes looked briefly at his face, which was grimly set.

She touched his arm and murmured, "Make sure he is unarmed and question him on Robert's whereabouts. I think I saw another shadow split off up the road just before." They pulled back from the window as the pair got close enough for them to see which entrance they would use: the front. Agnes went back into the room with the pallet while the three men ranged themselves around the top of the stairs behind curtains and doors.

The seconds ticked by until finally the squeak of metal hinge on wood door was heard below. Then the squeaks of the floor and the regular ones of the stairs. The stocky man came first, holding the wrist of the young woman behind him. He let go of it and got out a set of keys to unlock the sleeping room.

Barton burst from his hiding place and rushed at the man's head from behind. Horace joined in. By the time Henry had ducked in to get more sheets with which to restrain him, Barton had his elbow at the man's neck and Horace had his arms around his chest, pinning his arms to his side.

Henry pulled a knife from his boot and held it to the man's belly, which stopped him struggling.

"Let go the neck," breathed Henry. He handed the sheet to Barton to tie his hands, as he moved the knife to the man's throat.

"Now, man, what's your name?"

Something emerged that sounded like,

"Lock-in-a-bar."

"What's that?"

"Lock-na-gar," he repeated.

"All right, Locknagar, can you tell us what you're doing here at this early hour?"

"Seein' ay lady to 'er friends, as I 'as told," said Locknagar. It was an obvious bluff.

"Is that so," said Henry, making it flat—more of an accusation than a question. They all glanced over to the doorway where the young woman was standing as she'd been left, head down and body swaying slightly.

"Who was with you on the road earlier?"

The man became very stiff, and replied, "Twarn't no one else."

"There are three of us and one of you," Barton said. "Tell us the truth."

The man shuffled his feet, his hands tied behind him at the wrist and elbow, but said nothing.

Barton stepped out from behind the man, drew back his arm, and punched him solidly in the face. He fell back a few steps and Barton stepped forward, pushing him down onto the floor by the shoulders, where he landed sideways with a thump.

"Are you married, man? Do you have daughters? Do you know what is going on here?" Barton hissed.

Locknagar's nose had started bleeding, and he shook his head trying to clear it of the shock of the blow.

"No," he said. "Ent married. Don't know nothin'."

At that moment, the door beside them swung slightly inward and Agnes showed herself in the doorway. She did not move any closer to the four of them near the back wall. She looked at the man trussed and bleeding.

"Please just tell us where he's gone, sir. He needs to be stopped. All this," she motioned around herself, "needs to come to an end."

The man turned his head away from her appeal. He looked ashamed but did not offer any information.

"They're kidnapping young women—and men too, Locknagar. They're hypnotizing them and sending them out to do murder and assassination. Would you be a party to all that?" Henry asked.

"Just tell us," Barton broke in, "if the man whom you left—who paid you—does his name begin with a C?"

The man's head fell further down. "Aye,' came the muttered reply. "Chatsworth it is."

Horace leaned forward. "Where was he headed?"

The man shrugged.

"Not leaving again today, then," said Horace. "Where will he travel to next? Do you know that?"

"He bide here a while atwixt trips," said Locknagar.

"Well then," said Horace, "I suppose it is time we went back to pay father and son a visit."

Chapter 61

They woke the new girl from her trance easily by clapping and questioned her. She was luckily still in possession of her own memory. She did not know anyone in Aberdeen, being from Buckinghamshire, but a solution was found when they departed the house and met up with Jed, Barton's fisherman friend. Locknagar was left tied in the empty house. The new girl, whose name was Wanda, stayed with Diana and Ellen at Jed's mother's cottage with the understanding that their testimony at a trial might be needed if the others actually managed to catch Chatsworth this day. They were safely out of the way.

Barton, the MacFarlanes, and Agnes traveled on to the nearest inn on the outskirts of the village They were keyed to a high pitch of excitement but knew they must augment their strength before assembling a plan and acting on it.

The ostler's inn accepted the foursome without question, knowing from long experience that what its guests wanted was peace and no raised eyebrows. They sat in a booth next to the wall to eat and discuss how best to snare this wicked young man.

"I still think we should storm the gates at Chatsworth's estate," said Horace. "The father knows the truth and can no longer stand behind the boy. Boy," he scoffed. "Full-grown man—and a villain."

"But what of the guards, Horace? They did not let us in even when we were respected strangers," Henry said. "We can no more storm a gate than enter through the keyhole."

"Did you notice a servants' entrance when you were on the premises?" asked Barton.

Both shook their heads.

"What if you lured him out?" Agnes asked.

"How could we do it? He will be suspicious, or his father may yet want to guard his safety and tell him we are on to him," said Henry.

"Perhaps if it was someone he has not seen, calling on an errand for another…" She looked at Barton. "Yes, you could pretend to be a messenger from that Locknagar who needs something urgently. Unless there is already an agreed-upon procedure to go to someone else, in which case it would make him suspicious," she finished.

"You have a good seed of an idea there, Agnes," said Henry. "What else would lure him out but not cause suspicion? What else do we know of him?"

"That he's a scoundrel and gets into worse debts with his parties than I do gambling," said Horace, "Which, apparently, he finances through these illicit activities! What if we attempted to extort him, as he has done us?"

"Do you think he would believe you had discovered his secret?" Barton asked. "Or would you be too deeply implicated to be above suspicion yourself?"

Henry replied, "Too deeply in, I believe."

Barton said, "Well, I've got an idea for an urgent errand for that Locknagar," and he signaled the barkeep for some writing implements. He related it to Henry, who sketched out the barb with which to bait the enemy.

Agnes asked Barton whether or not they could safely involve the police at this point.

"We certainly should. The trick will be to have Chatsworth's villainy witnessed and confessed to by another policeman, in case Ragby tries to discredit me to save his own hide," Barton said, then murmured, "Excuse me."

Agnes touched his arm to draw his eyes to her, showing her gratitude for his efforts. He covered her hand briefly with his own, and cleared his throat.

"The trick is to find the right witnesses," he

said. "I shall need to find some policemen that are clean as a whistle and able to be trusted with our lives." He turned to Horace, who was muttering something to Henry over his shoulder and hadn't heard him.

"MacFarlane, how should we execute this plan? Will one of you go to deliver the message? Shall I go to find the police witness?"

"Police?" said Horace. "Who said we could involve that nasty bunch of—excuse me, Detective, but I think we've found that you are quite an exception on the force in your hold on your integrity."

"That may have been your experience in Carknocke County, sir, but I'm sure there must be some who are willing to do their duty. They are not all bad, sir."

"Could you find one or two not involved with the Chatsworth business before 10 o'clock tomorrow?" Horace asked. "I think we should deliver the missive early in the day and give him time to mull over the possibilities before we meet him tomorrow at nightfall. What do you think?"

"In that case," replied Barton, "I have until nightfall. We shall split up. I shall take Agnes to a new hotel where she can rest. Then I shall pay a visit to the district office, to try a test I shall devise. You, in the interim, can return to our original hotel and act at leisure, sending our letter, sleeping away the effects of the night, and readying your meeting location. Provided, that is, that the walls have been repaired after—is it yesterday's?—work." Barton smiled tiredly. "So, have you a good location in mind?"

"Hmm," replied Horace. "How is St. Mary's Church? That might be a good place to seem neutral, and if there is a balcony, witnesses could be stowed there."

"You will have to investigate, for I do not know, and you must decide the location before you send the note. Therefore, let us scatter now. We shall repair to the Gladwick Inn," he said, indicating Agnes and himself. "I spied it in my wanderings on the south side of the river. And you shall go to your investigating and letter-writing. You can send a message to us about the location for nightfall, where we will be safely cached an hour before." He turned to Agnes. "You may stay at the Gladwick; it would be safer for you."

"I would rather see him caught and hear his guilt with my own ears, if it does not endanger your safety," she replied. "I believe I can withstand it."

"Very well," said Barton. They all looked at one another, a flush creeping into some of their visages as they warmed to their task. Impulsively, Agnes put her hand in the middle of the table, looking around. She said, "Thank you for all of your aid. I wish you success, and luck, and that Providence be on your side." They all piled their hands together, one on another, prayed a silent prayer, and then the short spell was broken.

The MacFarlanes rose, tipped their hats to Agnes, and departed.

* * *

For a few minutes after they had left, the pair stayed at their table, Agnes gazing at her mug, Barton gazing at her. He waited.

Finally she stirred and glanced at him, then away. "Do you truly know any whom we can trust? I take it from Mr. MacFarlane's remark that Sergeant Ragby is positively not among that number?" she asked.

"No," Barton replied. "He is not. He tried to recall me from investigating the case back in Leeds. I am now, according to policy, acting on my own and entirely without authority." A pause. "But I think there are others like myself who are untainted and would volunteer to help when we tell them the case."

"But what will happen to you, even if we trap this man, his guilt is made known, and he is put away?" Agnes asked.

"I'm not sure but I think I shall be redeemed once I plead my case as part of the whole in front of a judge."

"A judge? You will have to plead your innocence then, just as this vile criminal will likely do? You, who have miraculously stuck by me... I am sorry for it," Agnes finished, her eyes full of pity and gratitude meeting his.

"I am not," said Barton. "For it has been worth every shred of my reputation and career to have you back safe and unharmed." He reached for her hand, pressed it warmly, and let go. "That man —the man we buried," he said, lowering his voice to below a whisper, "that may cause some difficulty but I will have to own it—and own it was self-defense in the line of duty." He lapsed into reverie. "But it shall be the first time for me. It is as yet... hard to think on."

"Then think of the four of us: four victims you have released from prison today," Agnes said. She reached back for his hand. She sought to convey her gratitude and indeed, her heart was in her mouth and the tears stood in her eyes as she realized the tenuous nature of his position.

"I will plead for you," she said.

Barton bathed in the glow of her gaze. He didn't know how to proceed but wanted to further this feeling in his chest, to give it voice.

"I have grown to appreciate your many qualities as I have worked to solve the mystery of you, Agnes," he started, his voice again at a low whisper. "I have learnt much about myself in the solving of it as well. I may say now that we are so close to—to an ending of some kind. But I would have you know that my acting in this case has not been wholly unbiased and without prejudice, for I believe from our meeting at Clatteringshaws I have harbored an—an admiration for you."

He looked at her quickly but she didn't move. He continued, "I know this to be an entirely unseasoned time and unlooked-for admission, and unorthodox in the extreme in terms of courting but I wanted you to know it. Your bravery and fortitude and goodness all show me more than any name and background could that you would be a most worthy companion, and—wife, if I could be so bold. When you disappeared at the road hotel, I was much more dismayed than I had any right to be, knowing you so little. But you have impressed me, Agnes, and— I am not in a position to ask you anything, my place being so uncertain, but I wanted you to know my honest feelings. There, I shall stop and give you a chance to answer."

Agnes smiled, causing two tears to race down. She reached with the back of her fingers to graze his cheek. "Gerard," she said. "I shall wait to return you my answer only so that it can be more proper and I can be released from this thing that torments me. I wish to be freely myself to speak with you. I am also in a very uncertain position. I know my own feelings toward you are honest and true, and I cannot say how I would have withstood this day were it not for you... We will wait, but not without knowing there is something to wait for."

She dashed away the tears and their tracks, recovering her composure as Barton also straightened, somewhat aglow.

Agnes asked, "Now who will be at the police station, or do you know somewhere else to go?"

* * *

He did. Barton escorted Agnes to the new hotel, then went to meet Jed to ask who was considered the most trustworthy of law officials in the town, immune to corruption. He was directed to a small house near the center of the south side of town. As he looked at the front door, wondering how to proceed, it opened and he found himself facing a large woman, solidly built and with a broom in her hand.

"Fitya dee'in, ya?" she asked.

He took a few steps forward so as not to shout. "I was referred to your house," he said. "Is your husband the retired magistrate Mr. MacLachlan?" At her inscrutable expression, he merely continued. "He was suggested to me as one in this town beyond reproach in judgement and honesty. I have a matter for which his help is much needed."

After a long minute in which she scrutinized him, she drawled, "Verra well. If ye say it, I'll believe it. Ye've a straight look about ye," and waved him in.

She invited him to sit in the small front parlor and she ducked through to the back of the building. Barton then heard her loud steps going up stairs. Presently, she reappeared with a bent old gentleman behind her, his white hair grown long and pulled back into a queue, his garments looking quaint but clean. Barton wondered if the man was a Quaker, but thought that odd in these parts. He stood as they entered.

The old man dragged the only other chair in the room, a wooden straight-backed one, opposite Barton and sat. He nodded to the woman, who then departed for the back again.

Before speaking, the gentleman gazed out the sheer window curtains for a few moments.

"All right, then," he said, finally. "What's afoot? I'm tol' ye've coom fer aid."

"Yes, Mr. MacLachlan, I have. To be very short about the situation, there has been a crime ring operating in the country for several years that we have discovered—and by we, I mean some associates of mine who were intended to be victims in the scheme. We believe we have found the instigator of the scheme and we intend to capture him this day so he can no longer perpetrate the kidnappings and crimes and—other things to which he subjected his victims.

"We have little information on his accomplices, who indeed have been trickier to follow, but we believe we can at least stop a large arm of the operations here by capturing him." He paused and wondered if it would be wise to mention the name —not yet.

"I became involved in this investigation as a member of Her Majesty's Police Force but I have discovered some corruption in the ranks which may call into question my actions in the future. That is why I am seeking an irreproachable witness for this stage," Barton said.

"How d'ye plan a' capture 'im?" the man asked. "And who is it ye're after?"

"Well, sir, we were hoping for your help in rounding up some constables whom you trust to hear this man's confession of complicity and guilt. Once that is accomplished, they would arrest him. It is Robert Chatsworth, sir."

A cackle erupted from the wrinkled face. "Begod if that ent true… well, I shall hear more of your story then and join with you. And to ask true —who was't that told ye to come t'me? Not Chisholm, was it?"

"No, sir. I know him by the name Jed Harper," said Barton.

Another cackle. "Begod and a wonder. I put awa' his father for stealing. Hmph," he said, considering things.

In a few more minutes, Barton had departed, with the promise to send a note about the location for their meeting an hour before nightfall.

MacLachlan charged himself with finding the constables.

Chapter 62

That afternoon, the message had been sent from the MacFarlanes: they would convene at the bakery toward the end of the east road out of town. The bakers would be asleep in the next building at dusk because of their schedule, and the bakery itself had plenty of nooks and crannies in which to hide and from which to observe.

When Barton and Agnes arrived, MacLachlan was already there with two men who were not in uniform but bore the ramrod backs and frowning expression of those who take themselves very seriously. They did turn a kindly eye to Agnes, whose story they must have heard.

Introductions were made among the men. Lewis and Parrish were the names of the Aberdonian police. Agnes did not give hers.

Horace arrived: the advance guard. He explained how they had made sure Robert Chatsworth would come. Horace had dressed shabbily and sent up a badly scrawled note from the gate of the estate that said an unexpected event had happened at the rooms and a decision was required from the boss.

That would plant many seeds in the boss's mind—Violence? Death? Discovery?—and meeting as far away from the ferry buildings as the bakery was meant to give Chatsworth the feeling of safe cover and not draw attention to the house holding the prisoners. No word had been returned but Horace felt sure he would take the bait.

McLachlan and the constables heard all this. They'd been given a sketch of the plot and the plan of capture and each thought about what the confession might reveal.

The elder Aberdonian gentleman had been the one thoughtful enough to bring some provisions. While the party waited—cached in different spots behind baking trays, under counters, and between large bins containing flour—a thick wedge of cheese and lammas bread was passed around, each confederate wetting his lips and chewing slowly to pass the tense time.

Some minutes later, a tread could be heard near the front door. It scuffed its shoes and opened the door quietly, pressing upward as it started to squeak on its hinge.

It was Henry's head that they saw, the hair messed and the face blacked with coal haphazardly, or so it seemed.

He entered and glanced around then closed the door behind him and said, "I can see the white of your jacket, sir; you would do better to find a different spot."

Lewis, with his sleeves showing a stripe of white fabric that lined the cuff, stepped out and bowed. He made eye contact with MacLachlan, and nodded. He changed positions and squatted back down.

"The sun is just set and it shall be dark in a quarter of an hour," Henry said. "Be prepared."

"Let it work," Barton murmured.

* * *

The last glow and reflection of the sun's rays had died and there was a breeze floating into the bakery; the sea wind off the shore smelled of cold weather to come and the city's other industry: jam-making. It was a striking combination for an out-sider, but one Lewis and Parrish heartily enjoyed when the wind was right.

No one heard the tread but all eyes were trained on the door as it opened inward. In came a medium-height man, his chestnut hair mostly covered by a plaid cap and the rest of him covered in a navy blue wool coat. What was visible of his face showed a patchy complexion—probably choler, Agnes thought, from her vantage point—a curling mustache, and a dominant upper jaw. Not a hand-some man but what could have been endowed with good looks by a kind demeanor was instead frozen with a look of apprehension and annoyance.

"Where are you?" he snapped.

Henry stepped forward. "Sor," he drawled.

"What has happened?"

"Sor, jes' this. I noticed one they ladies is in the family way, sor. Twarn't me, and Lochnagar denies it too. So what's t'be done about her?"

Chatsworth paused a moment. "Which one? Do you know their names?"

"Aah, not to be too sure, but…" Agnes willed Diana's name at him. "War it Diane? I think it was so."

"Diana," Chatsworth sighed. He cast a sharp eye at Henry. "How did you discover it?"

"Ach, she been sickly mornings for weeks, an' Lochnagar, he said he saw it as she was… movin' aboot," he finished.

Chatsworth kept his own counsel as he obviously pondered whether the offspring could be his and what he would do about it. Agnes watched and let her rage seethe.

She'd remembered his voice.

"Will ye be sendin' 'round for oon o' the doctors in the yard, then, sor?" Henry was trying to frame it ambiguously, so that Chatsworth might go with either his doctors the hypnotists or the doctors that do away with babies. He was balanced precariously now, making references he hoped would draw incriminating words.

"The yard?" said Chatsworth, turning his head to eye Henry's figure more fully. "What is your name?"

"My name—name's Mitchell," he said, pulling at his workpants with his fingers.

"How many damned people has MacNab brought into this affair?"

"Jes' me, sor. And Lochnagar, o'course. We're noon of us telling, sor. You can belie' that."

Chatsworth rubbed his chin and paced back and forth within a few feet, musing. Evidently he'd made a decision on something for he stopped and said, "I shall claim her as my mistress. Leave her in a trance so we don't worry about her leaving. I shall set her up in a cottage behind our lower pastures and have one of you order the necessaries to keep her for a while… yes."

Agnes listened to this and felt a glittering flush through her whole body. His voice recalled at once the lies he had told her in order to hypnotize her. She felt the weight of her loneliness, the uncertainty, the incapacity of her last year and more. All the work she had done to recall her memory and start anew with purpose, all the self-torture she had been through wondering what she'd done to deserve this fate—she recognized his voice from when they had met at a train station… it must have been when she was first taken. Now she remembered.

"And the others, sor? He didn't tell me nor when anyone'd come or when they be leaving."

"No. That's because he doesn't know until I tell him, the good man. Same for you. I have not yet learned what is to be their purpose and so there they stay. Is that clear?"

"Is that enough?" Henry returned in his normal voice, still looking at Chatsworth, straightening from the subservient crouch to his normal straight-backed position.

"Aye, I believe so," answered MacLachlan, emerging from the shadows of the oven hutch. At his appearance, Parrish leapt to the door to block the exit and Lewis rushed from the other side with a pistol aimed right at Chatsworth's ear.

"What in God's name is this?" Chatsworth asked. "You!" he said, pointing a finger at Henry, "What lies have you been telling? This is utterly ridiculous—"

He stopped as Agnes stepped out from the flour bins. She gazed at him piercingly and he was at first jarred by seeing a woman there but then the calculation that it must be one of his conquests, escaped and rebelling, flitted across his face. He did not recognize her face; she could see it.

"You," she breathed. "You were coming from some gay occasion, obviously in a hurry not to have changed. I was traveling home from visiting my mother's relatives, north of the city. I was returning home to be married!"

Agnes grew more emotional as these lines from her memory surged up within her; the word 'married' came out with a ragged edge.

"I was two years in service outside Glasgow, gone to visit relatives of my mother's down Lanarkshire way and was returning to be married to Mr. Hedley...but I never returned, did I?"

Chatsworth seemed struck dumb and tried badly to conceal his amazement at the tale unfolding before him. Lewis kept his pistol trained on him.

"I was spoken to by a fashionable gentleman at a middle stop as we paused. Fashionable but depraved. You hyp—" she hiccupped in her excitement, "kidnapped and hypnotized me then," she ground out. Her features were twisted in anger and as she drew a steadying breath she tried to settle them back into place. She glared at Chatsworth and noticed his expression had changed from one of amazement to feigned astonishment. He would denounce her, then. Agnes was not worried, not with the audience that she had.

"But now I have it back, I shall no longer be troubled by that memory. I shall step away from that period as one does when a horse has soiled the street. But you shall not." She subsided in her demeanor, relinquishing the power of holding the group's attention to another. Chatsworth promptly took it up in the theme she had anticipated.

"I am sorry if this raving woman has experienced hardship but you cannot believe she is sane? That I am at all connected with her misfortune? Gentlemen, come to your senses. She is obviously a lunatic!"

"I am as much a lunatic as you are an innocent man," said Agnes. "But you could help your case with all of us if you told us of the part Zemlya i volya plays in this."

He was visibly shaken on hearing the name but tried to brush it off. He looked around the room, obviously attempting to appeal to someone with the tale of her madness, but found only hard eyes and unforgiving faces.

"In order to prove that she is not in her right mind, I will engage my lawyer to attend to this matter. Put that away," Chatsworth said to Lewis, gesturing at the pistol.

"I will not. You will put out your arms," returned the constable.

"This is so ridiculous that I really cannot credit it. Are any of you police of Her Majesty's service? I doubt it. I will leave without being molested, or my father shall speak to the Lord Mayor —"

"We've already been to see your father, Chatsworth, and we have him quite convinced that you're a scoundrel. I would not look there for help. Put out your arms," said Horace.

Chatsworth narrowed his eyes at Horace, taking in the upper-class accent and the well-dressed form. It took a moment, but then his eyes widened, and hardened again as he realized his identity.

"Unbelievable! A MacFarlane, here in my backyard, trying to poison my reputation!"

At this he raised his right arm in gesticulating. Lewis grabbed it, followed by Henry—the next closest—who grabbed his other hand, forcing it behind his back. Parrish pulled out the hand-cuffs and fastened them to his wrists. Chatsworth spluttered and spewed obscenities at Horace, threatening action.

Horace promptly kicked him in the midsection, causing him to double over and try to regain his breath. In the quiet, he turned to MacLachlan, who said a cart was on its way; the whistle had been given. Horace continued to watch the now-prisoner on the floor and Lewis slipped outside to guide in the cart.

In a rush, everything was over. The villain was captured; someone else would have to deal with his misdeeds. Agnes felt the magnet that was opposing her being abruptly drawn away; she seemed to lose her strength for a moment. She put her hand on the wall to steady herself and became aware of Barton coming close. Henry, black-faced and scruffy as he was, also came over to see how she fared.

"We had better clear out of here as soon as possible—after he's been taken to the jail," said Henry. "We will likely have a harrowing several months now making sure Chatsworth is convicted and goes to prison for what he's done."

"No hope of his implicating any of his hypnotist colleagues, I suppose," said Horace sourly.

They looked to Barton, who was ready to catch Agnes if she were to keel over. Henry touched his shoulder.

"Well done, and thank you." Barton spared him a glance of acknowledgement.

He turned to Agnes, kneeling down to peer up into her face. "Well done, and thank you most of all. We will continue to pursue the linkages with Zemlya i volya, as well as we can. Are you well, for the moment?"

Agnes dragged her head up, which seemed impossibly heavy. She looked at Henry, so many thoughts swirling past her. "Yes. I will see him carted off and then retire to sleep. For several days if necessary," she added. "You played your role with great aplomb, sir," she said, regaining some liveliness. "You must have trod the boards before."

Henry smiled at her brave display, glad to see that her strength was not completely spent.

The squeak of the door opening and the growl from the man on the floor broke up the scene.

The cartman helped Lewis and Horace to put Chatsworth in the cart. It had special wooden sides seven feet high to prevent escape.

The Aberdonians accompanied the prisoner to the jail, accompanied by the out-of-towner Mac-Farlanes. Barton walked Agnes slowly on the path away from the baker's shop in the chilly evening air.

Chapter 63

"Are you well enough to take a meal back at the Gladwick? I think some food and wine would help restore you," Barton asked as they walked along.

"I think so. At any rate, it is a good idea," replied Agnes. "It is as if all my frustration and anger from the past year and more was boiled down to the past hour and given release. Very good for the soul but very taxing also." She smiled briefly.

"That is well," Barton murmured, and let them lapse into silence as she leaned on his arm and they slowly wound their way back to the hotel.

Barton's mind darted to and fro as he imagined how the police would consider the case—his case—and whether he would continue a career as an investigator. On the one hand, he had diligently done his duty; on the other, he had killed and buried a man in secret and threatened some very powerful individuals. Thoughts of his sergeant made him pause. Did they in fact have any evi-

From girl w no past
to woman w no future

dence upon which to accuse him, or Worley? Perhaps Worley was right, and they would simply be allowed to carry on as though Agnes had never stumbled into their web of deceit. He thought of the Aberdonians who had come to their aid that evening and blessed their souls.

He hoped fervently Agnes might be spared a long, open, drawn-out trial, but how else would they attract attention to find the political radicals responsible for the whole reprehensible operation? He couldn't slow his thinking and the questions zig-zagged around his head.

Agnes, meanwhile, had successfully blocked out the future. She felt her weight leaning on the policeman's arm, and the soles of her feet touching the road they walked but intentionally kept her mind dark for this small interval. Having had a glimpse of the police's view of interrogation and investigation, she did not want to experience the ordeal in advance by worrying about it. She did not attempt to piece together all the events so that they would hang together neatly—yet.

She forbore wondering about Barton's fate: something which had touched her heart earlier but which was beyond her capacity to consider at the moment. She enjoyed his arm and the road rising to meet her feet; she held all thoughts back until she could regain the reserves to stand her ground against them.

They reached the Gladwick and sat for a late meal in the dining room. She ate very slowly and he succeeded in likewise pushing away the questions for a time, delighting in looking at her content face. It seemed washed-clean as he had never yet seen it, different from her usual schooled expression.

As they dined, a rider arrived with a note for them from Henry MacFarlane. It read:

Dear sir and madam,

The power of the right witnesses, found by the power of honest connections, has triumphed over thievery and knavery, and he is safe in jail for the time being. The father, I believe, will prove our ally in his prosecution but is useless in the pursuit of the Z i V. We shall nevertheless alert contacts in the places who monitor such things of all we know, and both of you may be called upon in the future on that account as well as the more individual crimes.

You must both rest up, as we will be doing. MacLachlan has heard all the relevant details we know and will pass as lightly as possible over the initial instigation for our involvement. We hope the police here will call us when it comes to witnesses for earlier events but intend to return to as normal lives as we may find. We also intend to aid Det. Barton in restitution of duty and clearance of any suspicion.

H and I send our best wishes to you this night. We will come to see you tomorrow in the afternoon, if you are sufficiently recovered to receive guests. We remain forever your devoted servants, and friends,

H. M. the Elder

Barton read it aloud in low tones, then passed it to Agnes.

"Let us hope they succeed in clearing your name," said Agnes.

"As normal lives as we may find," repeated Barton. "Yes, and I wonder how normal that will be. You will want to return to your home? Your— Mr. Hedley? I am sorry, Agnes." He couldn't bring himself to tell her what had happened with the fiancé, not at the moment.

"I will write a letter in the morning," Agnes said briskly, and then stifled a yawn. "For now I can do nothing but sleep. I—I need to have some time to myself, and then yes, I think I will go to Glasgow. But no more thinking until I have rested."

They rose and Barton bid her good-night at the staircase. She turned to him to say, "I would be very happy if you could come to Glasgow with me, you who have fought for and protected me, trusted my word, and valued my thoughts from the beginning."

"I will do it," said Barton. "I will be there."

Chapter 64

After several days of rest and a flurry of express letters to Agnes' old Glasgow neighborhood of Maryhill, she was escorted there by Barton. She went to her old home alone to find her mother alive and her father sickly, as she now remembered was the case. Her sister and two brothers were still living in their home parish. They reacted as if they'd seen a ghost at first but were only too overjoyed to welcome her back, even accepting her new chosen name without question. So Effie became Agnes; then, she asked the nerve-wracking question.

"What's become of the arrangement with Mr. Hedley, Mother?"

"Oh, well, that! He came to see us about six mun' after ye disappeared and heartbroken as we all were, we had to release 'im, ye understand? He's been married now almost a year to Gretchen doon the glen. We all thought you were dead, m'dear," her mother said, curling a lock of hair around Agnes' ear. "I am sorry to've done it now, but—"

"It's all right, Mother. I think I've found a better match." And she smiled a small smile. She would tell her mother and sister about Gerard in another day or two once they had some of their old ways back in place.

The details of the trial's investigations hung over Agnes. She and Gerard traveled back to Aberdeen for several weeks. The police paid for Barton's sojourn, and the MacFarlanes for Agnes'. They were disappointed to see no linkages with the Zemlya i Volya brought to justice, but then they also knew that their man Ellers would be hot on their trail—wherever they were in the Empire.

At the end of that time, difficult but punctuated with joy, they journeyed south to meet each other's families. Even though this was the second time for Barton, he experienced everything in a different light entirely.

Barton would settle at Stirling, a place between their two families, where a new institute for the investigative sciences was going to be opened. His new wife settled into her small household and made friends in the neighborhood: a great pleasure denied her for so long that she relished it now tenfold.

As the suits for Ragby and Worley wound

their ways through the court, the newly married Bartons were called upon as witnesses but were again frustrated by the lack of weight given to their testimony when compared with the word of the criminals themselves. Ragby was removed from service and posted elsewhere, so at least a small cog of the great machine of corruption was cut away.

Agnes made a visit to Lady Helen to tell her the story but found an empty house at Quebec Street. Stanley the valet told her that Lady Helen had removed to Clatteringshaws indefinitely. "For her nerves," he'd said. She did not try to reestablish contact.

From time to time, Agnes Barton was disturbed by dreams of her tenure as an operative agent of the Zemlya i Volya but these diminished as her new life became filled with other details, friendly faces, and a familiar routine in Stirlingshire. Her siblings, her country neighbors, her husband, she cherished them all. She had awoken to the brevity of life and she was determined to reach out and enjoy it.

Did you enjoy this book?

Please consider posting a review.

Reviews like yours help this book find its way into the hands of new, grateful readers. This helps self-published authors gain readers online and through word-of-mouth networks.

You are cordially invited to visit my author website at www.margaretpinard.com for blog posts, events, news, and giveaways. There will be helpful Bonus Content posted there for the *Remnants* series as well!

Reviews are much appreciated at Amazon.com, Goodreads.com, or any other review sites. Or spread the news through your own networks on Facebook and Twitter!

Good books should be shared.

My eternal thanks for your time, attention, and encouragement.

-Margaret Pinard

About the Author

Margaret Pinard has spent her first few decades traveling the globe in search of adventures to incorporate into her writing, including living in the lands of the Celts, the cities of European fashion, and several dolce far niente Mediterranean cultures.

Her favorite genre is historical fiction, and she especially delights in fiction that makes you feel like you've been transported to a different time and place. *Memory's Hostage* is her first novel. Her second, *Dulci's Legacy*, grew out of her first NaNoWriMo attempt in 2012. *The Keening* is the first in her new *Remnants* series. She resides in Portland, OR.

74241104R00201

Made in the USA
Columbia, SC
27 July 2017